I0616546

MY LUCKY GROOM

By
Ginny Baird

Published by
Winter Wedding Press

Edited by Linda Ingmanson
Cover by Dar Albert

About the Author

From the time that she could talk, romance author Ginny Baird was making up stories, much to the delight -- and consternation -- of her family and friends. By grade school, she'd turned that inclination into a talent, whereby her teacher allowed her to write and produce plays, rather than write boring book reports. Ginny continued writing throughout college, where she contributed articles to her literary campus weekly, then later pursued a career managing international projects with the US State Department.

Ginny's held an assortment of jobs, including school teacher, freelance fashion model, and greeting card writer, and has published more than ten works of fiction and optioned nine screenplays. She's additionally published short stories, nonfiction and poetry, and admits to being a true romantic at heart.

Ginny is the author of several bestselling romantic comedies, including novellas in her *Holiday Brides Series*. She's a member of Romance Writers of America (RWA), the RWA Published Authors Network (PAN), and the RWA Published Authors Special Interest Chapter (PASIC).

When she's not writing, Ginny enjoys cooking, biking and spending time with her family in Tidewater, Virginia. She loves hearing from her readers by email at GinnyBairdRomance@gmail.com and welcome visitors to her website at http://www.ginnybairdromance.com.

Prologue

Eleven-year-old Ventura Hart sat with her back to the ornate mirror. There was something unnatural about watching herself eat. Or maybe when she wasn't looking, she didn't have to worry she was eating too much. Her mom and skinny teenage sister were always on her case. Tuck down your collar, straighten that skirt, and for goodness sakes, Ventura, pin up your hair… But for now, here in this moment, Ventura didn't have to worry about any of that. She was with the one person who made her feel like a princess. Her father.

His handsome face creased with worry as he set down his chopsticks.

"You're not eating."

"I was just deciding," she admitted honestly, "if I should have some more."

He smiled pleasantly, heaping another serving of sesame chicken on her plate. "Of course you should have some more. A young girl…" He paused a moment, his temples reddening slightly. "Young woman like yourself, I mean, needs to keep her strength up."

Ventura grinned, thinking her face must look as bright as the pretty Chinese lanterns strung from the ceiling. This had to be the best night of her life. Her dad had never taken her on a date before. It was special having all of his attention for once, without having to share it with her competitive older sister. Not that Hope had to do much to compete. Just by being there, she somehow made herself seem better. She was smart and pretty, with long, straight, beautiful hair that made her look like she'd walked right off a television commercial. Their mom had stopped coming out to dinner with them a while ago. Ventura wasn't sure why but thought it had something to do with her new business. Ventura's mom was always starting a new *enterprise*, as she liked to call it. Ventura had actually won the fifth-grade spelling bee based on that word alone. She had her mom to thank for that, at least.

Her dad made easy conversation, asking about her friends in school and laughing warm-heartedly at her lame eleven-year-old jokes. Ventura tried to be as witty as he was but wasn't always sure her words came out right. She was determined to work on it, though. Someday she'd be just as glib as her well-spoken father. He wrote for a magazine, and she hoped that someday she would do that as well. It sure seemed a whole lot saner than starting a new enterprise every year or two.

Before Ventura was ready for their dinner to be over, a waiter appeared to clear their plates and deliver fortune cookies. "This was so much fun!" she told her dad eagerly. "Really great, just the two of us." She drew a breath, then pressed ahead with a hopeful gaze. "Maybe we can do it again?"

"Yes, well. Ventura…" He studied her kindly, then set his wallet on the table. He'd been about to pay their bill, but something had stopped him. Ventura's heart skipped a beat when she realized that whatever it was, it was likely bad news. He laid his hand on top of hers above the linen tablecloth. Ventura's palm pressed the pilled fibers, her entire universe plummeting. "I'm afraid, darling, that we won't be able to do this again for a long time."

"Why not?"

His dark eyes brimmed with sadness. "I've taken an assignment in Kenya."

"Kenya?" Ventura asked in shock. She didn't know exactly where that was but was fairly certain it was in Africa. On another continent entirely.

Her lips trembled slightly. "You mean, we're going there with you?"

He slowly shook his head. "No, sweetheart. I'm going alone."

Ventura withdrew her hand and clasped it in the other one in her lap atop her nubby wool skirt, the one that was short enough to wear with tights but long enough to hide her chubby knees. "But what about Hope and Mom, and—"

"That's the other thing I need to tell you. I'm very sorry if this is hard, Ventura, but your mother and I haven't been getting along for quite some time now. And we've decided to—"

He couldn't leave her. *He wouldn't.* She shut her eyes, the word coming out as a puff of breath: "No."

"We're getting divorced."

Ventura pursed her lips and counted to twenty-five. Twenty-five was a good number, because that was the age she would be when she was all grown up. She'd be her own person then, with no one to push her around, hurt her feelings—or break her heart. She opened her eyes and stared at her dad, her eyes bleary. "When do you go?"

"Tomorrow, I'm afraid."

Ventura recalled getting smacked in the stomach with a soccer ball and having the wind knocked out of her. This felt a thousand times worse. She forced herself to be calm and ignore the raging feelings inside her, the way she did when popular girl Melissa Perry taunted her on the bus. All she had to do was pretend that none of this was happening, and sooner or later, it would go away. "Okay."

"Okay?" Her dad leaned forward with a quizzical look. "Are you really all right with this? I mean, do you have any questions?"

Only about a billion, but she wasn't sure they would matter anyway. "Nope."

"Well, okay, then." He heaved a sigh, his tense face relaxing. "At least that's over with." He lifted the small plastic tray between them, offering up a shrink-wrapped crescent. "Fortune cookie?"

Ventura shrugged and took one off the tray, unwrapping it slowly and prying it open.

"Well?" he asked, forcing a smile in an effort to lighten the moment. "Come on, what does it say?"

Even at her tender age, the irony was not lost. She folded the narrow strip of paper neatly in half and tucked it in her pocket. "It doesn't really matter." But the truth was, it did. It mattered a lot.

Chapter One

Fourteen years later, Ventura adjusted her bulky frame in the cramped quarters of the booth, scanning job postings on the Internet. Her laptop was six years old and painfully slow with downloads and connections. She'd been awarded it along with her scholarship package to a small liberal arts school, then had gotten a full ride to a Master's program in writing from there. Unfortunately, the graduate school grant hadn't included a new computer.

A middle-aged woman in pearls and an eccentric summer hat strolled by, nearly tumbling over Ventura's suitcase. She reached down and slid it under the table, taking in the café's varied clientele. There had to be at least ten countries represented by the patrons, who ranged from a man in a turban to Asian college students with handhelds, and guys in pinstriped suits and dark glasses, who seemed just a little bit scary. Ventura caught the hint of a foreign tongue and noticed two slender African women dressed in headscarves, chatting merrily over coffee in the corner. Ah yes, this was Washington, DC. Land of opportunity. For her, she hoped.

Waitresses scrambled to keep up with the crowd, busily refilling drinks and carrying fresh orders out on trays. A stylish beauty in her mid-twenties with short, raven hair tilted a coffeepot toward Ventura's cup. Ventura looked up to thank her, noticing an incredibly hot guy taking a seat at a nearby table. He was built and blond, and looked like he'd just walked off the beach in California, although the suit and tie spelled Capitol Hill intern. He glanced her way, and Ventura smiled hopefully, her elbow knocking her cup just as the waitress poured. Hot Guy ignored her and grinned broadly at the server, who was now staring at him and about to miss Ventura's cup.

"Look out!"

The waitress righted the pot, but hot coffee cascaded down her fingers. "Ow! That hurt!" she shouted, quickly setting the pot on the table to grip her fingers.

Ventura jumped back as coffee splattered over the pot's rim, rushing toward her. She dammed its flow with a heap of napkins, saving her aging laptop just in time.

Hot Guy leapt to the rescue…of the cute waitress, of course. To him, Ventura was invisible. She watched in amazement while he grabbed more napkins from the holder and heaped them on the mess. He dipped a clean one in Ventura's ice water, swabbing it over the girl's fingers.

"Are you okay?" he asked, still holding her hand.

The waitress reclaimed her fingers and examined them. "I think so." She passed the dripping napkin back to the guy and addressed Ventura. "I'm so sorry! Are you all right?"

Ventura nodded numbly, thinking this was always the way. For most of her life, she'd been completely discounted by men. She hadn't even had a boyfriend in high school. When guys took an interest, they considered her the girl with the good personality…and, she presumed—though none had specifically said—the great big butt.

"Here, let me help with that," Hot Guy said, his gaze locked on the server, who Ventura couldn't help but notice had a teeny tiny derriere, the kind they put in ads for women's sportswear. *Good gosh, he's practically drooling.* Ventura looked down with a start to find him absentmindedly sweeping soaked napkins off the table—right into her lap!

"Hey!"

The waitress shooed the guy away and nabbed the trash. "He's a real Einstein, that one," she said under her breath, rolling her eyes toward the guy, who reluctantly took his seat at the next table. In spite of herself, Ventura giggled. "Let me grab some fresh rags," the server told her apologetically. "I'll be right back."

She resurfaced quickly with some damp cloths and handed one to Ventura so she could wipe off her jeans.

"I totally apologize for the mess. Can I get you anything else? Some fresh coffee, maybe?"

Ventura glanced down at her clothing, grateful it would wash. She was pretty tight on money these days and had a limited wardrobe. "Thanks, I've already had mine."

The waitress shot her a wry smile. "Wise guy, huh?"

"Just the check, please."

"Oh no, you don't." She scribbled something on her pad and pressed the tab to the table. "This one's on the house. We don't charge for dumping on customers."

"Hey, as long as you've got your pen out…" The girls turned to look at Hot Guy, who unbelievably still had the nerve to talk to them. "Do you think I could have your number?" Naturally, Ventura noted, he was addressing the server, not her.

The server set her hand on her hip and stared at Hot Guy with incredulity. Ventura was impressed. She'd seen many a blow-off look, and this one *ruled*.

"Not even your cell?" he asked lamely.

The server shook her head and sighed heavily, turning back to Ventura. "I apologize for him too. None of that should have happened."

Ventura shrugged, resigned. "Happens all the time."

"What do you mean?"

"Oh, just that guys like *him*," she said as Hot Guy finally came to his senses and scurried out the door, "don't generally take an interest in girls like me. If you know what I'm saying."

The server crossed her arms and thoughtfully studied Ventura. "Might help if you lose the glasses."

"What?" Ventura asked in disbelief. She adjusted her tortoiseshell frames, thinking they suited her fine. In fact, she believed they'd won her extra points in graduate school. Everyone took a girl seriously who wore such serious-looking eyewear. The fact was, she did have contact lenses but rarely used them. She didn't really see the point.

"I'm just saying…" She nodded her head, appraising. "You actually have very pretty eyes. But this? Hoo boy." To Ventura's horror, she leaned forward, invading her personal space, and twisted up a curly mass of hair. "This, girlfriend, needs work."

Ventura blinked. "Excuse me?"

"You've got to *do* something with it. Not straighten it, I don't think. If I were you, I'd definitely go with the curl. Except for on special occasions. Then, I'd use a flat iron. Maybe add some highlights? Auburn to bring out the hint of red in your brown?"

Ventura gaped at her. "And you're such an expert because…?"

The server smiled proudly. "I'm getting my degree in fashion studies. Online." She scanned the bustling room, then leaned forward with a confidential whisper. "As soon as I'm done, I'm out of here. You know what I'm saying? O. U. T. Out. And onto a better life for myself."

"Um, that's great." Ventura gathered her things, preparing to stand.

The server stopped her, laying a hand on her arm. "What do you do?"

Ventura eyed her uncertainly. "I write."

"Cool! What kind of stuff? Would I know it?"

"Just obituaries, up until now."

"How depressing. Black isn't even in anymore."

"I'm looking for something better."

"More power to you. I'd imagine dead people aren't much fun." She extended her hand toward Ventura. "I'm Mary."

Ventura tentatively took her hand and shook it. "Ventura."

"Where are you headed with that suitcase of yours?"

"I'm new here, so I got a sublet temporarily. Maybe you can tell me which subway to take?" She shared a small piece of paper bearing a handwritten address.

Mary took the slip of paper and crumpled it in her hand. "Oh no, you don't. I'm not sending you there."

"Why not?"

"Are you kidding? What would you want with that location?"

"All the other places cost an arm and a leg."

"Yeah, well, this is where you go if you want to give your booty too." She fanned her face with her hand. "That's hot territory. Red-light district, baby."

Ventura's face fell. Here she was, a new girl in a new town, and she'd booked herself into a brothel.

Mary studied her a beat, taking pity. "Hey, don't look so down. You know what they say, *When God closes a door, he opens a disco.*"

"Window."

"What?"

"The expression is… Never mind."

"I really did mean to allude to a party."

"I'm not sure I know what you're saying."

"My landlady's looking for a new tenant."

"Are you serious?"

"As serious as a makeover." She studied Ventura with determination. "It's the perfect opportunity, for you and me both."

"What's in this for you?"

"If we don't find another girl by Monday, my rent doubles."

Ventura eyed her skeptically. "Where exactly is this place of yours?"

"On Capitol Hill. You'll love it. It's just Nanette, who's a little weird."

"Nanette?"

Mary shot her a big, bright grin. "You'll see."

The front door opened, and a flamboyant woman in her sixties greeted Mary warmly, then glanced at Ventura. Her red hair was spun up high in something akin to a beehive, and her brightly colored, polka-dot dress fit tightly over a curvaceous figure. She blinked behind long false lashes.

"Hello! What's this? A new makeover project?"

Mary protectively wrapped an arm around Ventura's shoulder and tugged her inside. Ventura nearly stumbled, dragging her suitcase behind her. "This is Ventura, our new boarder."

Nanette studied Ventura from head to toe, then back up again. "So you're a lucky girl, ha?"

Ventura was surprised Nanette knew the meaning of her name. Most folks just equated it with the song "Ventura Highway." Ventura forced what she hoped was a pleasant expression. "Not yet, but I'm trying."

"And we're going to help her," Mary said eagerly, shutting the door behind her.

"Hmm, yes. I see what you mean." Nanette narrowed her eyes. "Might help if we start with the hair."

Ventura swallowed hard, affronted. "Maybe this wasn't such a good idea," she told them both.

"Nonsense!" Nanette proclaimed with a wave of her hand. "Improving ourselves is *always* a good idea." She winked at Mary, sharing some private understanding, then turned her gaze back on Ventura. "Don't you worry one bit, dear. We'll do everything in our power to help. It certainly worked with the last girl."

"Last girl?"

"My roommate before," Mary explained. "She moved out to get married."

"That was *after* we helped her turn her life around."

"And her wardrobe," Mary inserted.

Hoo boy, just what have I gotten myself into? Ventura wondered. Her gaze traveled toward the door. There was still time to make her escape. But where would she go? Hotels in the city were expensive, and she barely had enough in savings for a security deposit and her first month's rent. Maybe it wouldn't be so bad. She could try it for the first month, then bolt if things got creepy.

"Why don't you take her to the basement, Mary? I'm sure Ventura's tired and would like to settle in."

Basement? Ventura stared around the cluttered living room decorated with heavy swags of velvet curtains, old stuffed furniture, and hurricane lamps that looked like they came from another century. Except these were electric. Ventura wondered briefly if there'd be a single lightbulb dangling from a string in the chamber below. Maybe above a solitary chair in the center of the room. The kind used for interrogating people. Or worse, for making over their hair.

"Come on," Mary urged, hoisting Ventura's heavy bag to help her. "Let me show you your new digs."

Ventura followed her down the dark staircase with trepidation. At least the neighborhood seemed nice, and the townhouse looked neat enough from the outside, with its red brick façade and beveled bay windows leading to a turret on top. But down here in the dungeon, there didn't appear to be a hint of natural light anywhere.

Mary flipped on a light, illuminating the small space. Ventura was relieved to see it wasn't nearly as horrid as she'd imagined. They'd entered a small efficiency kitchen with a checkerboard floor and a tiny Formica-topped table with chairs. Through a doorway into the main room, she found two neatly arranged twin beds separated from a living area by a large Oriental screen. Ventura spied blinking neon colors and walked toward the back of the room, mesmerized by the pulsating lights. Noting they streamed through a high transom window, she stood up on her tiptoes to peer out of it. Finally, thank goodness. Something that was bound to be an excellent sign. *Zen's Chinese Take-Out: Open Twenty-Four Hours.* What more could a girl hope for?

"So?" Mary asked. "What do you think?"

She turned toward Mary with a grin. "I'll take it."

An hour later, Ventura was nearly unpacked. Only the treasures in the front flap of her suitcase remained. She debated on whether to take them out, then reasoned Mary would understand. "Do you mind if I put a few things on the refrigerator?"

Mary looked up from where she sat on the bed painting each of her toenails purple and shrugged. "What you got in there?" she asked, indicating Ventura's bag. "A whole magnet collection?"

"That and a few fortunes." Ventura dug out a gallon-size plastic bag with a zippered seal. It was stuffed to the brim with little white slips of paper.

Mary set her polish bottle down on the nightstand with a thunk. "How long did it take you to eat all—I mean, collect those?"

"Been saving them for years."

"Really?" Mary's dark eyes lit up with interest. "Any special ones?"

"They're all special," Ventura told her. And they were. Each and every one had spoken to her in some individual way. Not that she was superstitious or anything.

"I mean, *extra special*," Mary prodded.

Even though there was one of particular importance, Ventura didn't know Mary well enough to share it with her. In fact, in all these years, she'd never shared it with anybody. Just kept it squirreled away in a secret spot in her wallet, so she could glance at it whenever she felt like it.

"Yeah," Ventura teased. "There's one about meeting a tall, dark stranger."

Mary's mouth fell open. "You're kidding! They still print that?"

"No. That one is vintage. At least ten years old. But I've got it." She dug it out of her bag as evidence and handed it over.

Mary laughed and shook her head. "You're funny, Ventura. You should come with me tomorrow. Meet some Washingtonians."

"Where are you going?"

"Some big arts fundraiser. Scored tickets from my friend Petra at the gallery."

"I'm not sure. It sounds…" Ventura looked down at her dowdy clothes. "Fancy."

"Tons of people will be there," Mary tempted. "Reporters and such. Maybe you can make connections?"

That sounded good in abstract. Concretely, Ventura wasn't sure she could pull it off. Attending some big DC soiree with tons of society types, on only her second day here?

Mary studied Ventura's clunky sandals. "Bring any better shoes?"

Ventura sat on the bed with a sigh. "They're all more or less like this."

Mary's face brightened sweetly. "No worries. We've got plenty of time."

Chapter Two

Ventura and Mary approached the awning overhanging the gold-framed front doors to the glitzy hotel. Arriving limousines were greeted by valets opening doors and escorting elegantly clad patrons into the night. Ventura clomped forward, self-consciously adjusting her too-tight halter. The dress might have been Lycra, but the tiny size eight was stretched to the max over Ventura's ample size-twelve figure.

"Stop gripping on to me, will ya?" Mary chided Ventura as she clung to Mary's elbow, teetering unsteadily on spiky heels.

"You should have let me wear flats."

Mary shot her an indignant pout. "I know that was a joke." While they were a different size in dresses, luckily for her, Mary had said, they both shared the same size shoes. "Come on," she said, leading Ventura along. "You look gorgeous."

Ventura tucked her cleavage beneath her glittery thigh-high gown. It was all gold and sparkly, making Ventura feel more like a bulbous Christmas ornament than a glam girl.

A bellman pulled back the door, and the women walked inside. Mary waved her tickets in the air with a smile and they headed for the ballroom door. "This is going to be fab. You'll see."

"Sure," Ventura said. "Just don't go too far. I might topple over."

Mary swatted Ventura's hand with the tickets. "Get a hold of yourself, and put on your party face. This is your big chance. An opportunity to mingle! Actually," she said, prying Ventura's fingers off her arm, "it's my chance too." Then, to Ventura's horror, she started to scurry away. "Catch you in a while. Ta!"

Ventura drew a breath, attempting to steady herself. The room in front of her was abuzz with clinking champagne flutes and society chatter. Men in tuxedos walked by, chatting amiably while elegantly coiffed women followed. A waiflike blonde threw her head back in exaggerated laughter, attempting to flatter a gorgeous, dark-eyed man. There were so many conversations milling about, it was impossible to pick up more than snippets of them beneath the clickity-clack of empty drink glasses being set down on trays as waiters carted fresh libations forth.

Suddenly, from across the room, she caught a man's gaze on her. He was to-die-for handsome with wavy dark hair and a toned, trim body packaged perfectly beneath his pressed white shirt and bow tie. Ventura judged him to be in his early thirties, and—she couldn't believe it—he was smiling at *her*. Ventura blinked hard, and the heavy mascara Mary had pasted on her lashes caused them to stick. She gasped and pried them apart just in time to see the heartthrob approaching.

"Can I help you find something?" He spoke with no hint of an accent, but his eyes were all dark and dreamy like he'd come from some exotic land. "You look a little lost."

She was lost all right. Hook, line, and sinker *sunk* in his hypnotically sexy gaze. "Huh?"

He angled his champagne flute in her direction. "Are you meeting someone?"

"No," she spouted quickly. "Just looking!" *Oh great, Ventura.* "Browsing!" *Worse.* "Um…" She bit into her bottom lip, feeling her cheeks blaze. "I'm new in town."

He chuckled good-naturedly and extended his hand. "Welcome to our fair city. I'm Richard."

She settled her palm in his grip, and a billion warm tingles raced down her spine. "Ventura," she answered weakly. Ventura pulled herself up short, realizing she sounded like some love-struck schoolgirl. She was grateful none of her professors had looked like *that*. She wouldn't have been able to get an ounce of work done. Apart from a little creative writing. Yeah, she could spin herself a tale or two involving herself and this unbearably hot man. The only trouble was, given the exciting details of Ventura's past, the story would be rated PG. Ventura sighed as he released her hand with a worried gaze.

"Are you all right?" he queried kindly. "You look like you should sit down."

Ventura imagined him sweeping her into his strong arms and carrying her across the crowded ballroom—then inwardly slapped her silly face. "I'm fine," she said hastily. "Just catching my breath after the long walk here."

"Where from?"

"Capitol Hill."

He glanced down at her spiky high heels, then once more met her eyes. "I'm impressed."

Just then, Ventura spied Mary approaching with a pert brunette with springy curls. Of all the people she wanted to see now, her beautiful apartment mate was at the bottom of the list. And the girl with her was just as pretty. Mary whispered something to her friend, then caught Ventura's eye, beaming brightly. She carried an extra flute of champagne, which she raised in a silent toast as she drew near.

"There you are, you devilish man!"

Ventura turned in surprise to see a trim redhead had sidled up next to Richard and linked her arm through his. Was it Ventura's imagination or did he seem to stiffen at her approach? "I've been looking for you *everywhere*."

He patted her arm and answered mildly, "We're supposed to talk with the guests. That's what this event's all about." Ventura wasn't sure what Richard's role was in things, but she figured him to be one of the gala's organizers. From what Mary had told her, a wealthy Washington benefactor had established a fund to raise college scholarship money for students studying the arts. Money from tickets purchased to attend this event would go toward that cause. A number of local organizations had purchased them in bulk as a sign of good will. Petra had been lucky enough to get three of them as gifts from her employer without paying a cent.

"I'm Petra," the bouncy brunette said, cozying up to the group.

Mary handed her extra champagne flute to Ventura, then addressed the others. "And I'm Mary."

Richard politely bowed his head in greeting, acknowledging them both. "Richard."

The redhead sighed and rolled her eyes. "Monica," she said, giving Richard's arm a small tug.

Richard glanced at Monica, then said apologetically, "I'm afraid duty calls."

"Of course," Ventura said.

"It's been very nice meeting you." He pleasantly surveyed their faces, then settled his gaze on Ventura. "I hope we have the pleasure again."

Ventura's heart skipped a beat as she felt her temperature spike. Was Richard really focusing all his attention on *her?*

"Me too." She tried to say it boldly, but her words came out as a whisper.

Then he turned and walked away, with Monica scolding him soundly over something Ventura couldn't quite overhear and which Richard seemed to ignore.

"Richard Blake," Mary said once he was out of earshot. "In the flesh."

Petra rapidly fanned her face with her hand. "I'd like to see that."

"Of course you would," Mary told her. "You and every other woman in Washington." She turned to Ventura. "How did you do it?"

"What?"

"Get him to come over and talk to you?" Petra filled in.

"I just stood here," Ventura offered, still amazed by the turn of events herself. She normally wasn't much of a man magnet and had never attracted anyone quite as dishy as Richard. Of course, maybe she hadn't attracted him at all. As one of the hosts, it was his role to work the room. "I'm sure he was just being gracious."

Mary studied her proudly. "Must be the hair."

Ventura self-consciously fingered her flat-ironed locks, which made her whole head feel as if it were wearing a weighty wig.

"I like it!" Petra proclaimed. "Maybe you can do mine sometime?"

"You've done good, Ventura," Mary told her. "Schmoozing with the District's most eligible bachelor."

"Every woman in the world wants to date him," Petra added.

Ventura's gaze followed Richard across the room as he and his girlfriend made the rounds. "Monica seems pretty well settled in."

"Her?" Mary asked with a laugh. "She's just his escort."

"What do you mean?"

"The latest in a long line of girls," Petra explained. "He never attends these society things alone."

"And is never seen with a woman outside of them," Mary added.

Ventura took a sip of her champagne, its bubbles tickling her tongue. "But why?"

"Might have to do with the kids," Mary said confidentially.

Petra nodded. "Or the ex."

"She was terrible." Mary lowered her voice. "Walked out on him and two babies."

Petra whispered behind her hand, "They're rumored to be brats."

"They dress well," Mary argued defensively.

Petra shook her head. "Fashion's not everything."

Mary's eyes flashed in horror. "Bite your tongue!"

Later that night, Ventura found herself in bed but totally unable to sleep. What *was* that thumping coming from upstairs? "What's going on up there?" she asked as flashing neon colors pulsed through the window.

"That's Nanette practicing her Lambada," Mary answered.

"Lam… What?"

"It's some kind of crazy dance she does. She'd got a ton of them and will try to teach you if you're not careful."

"I'll take your advice and steer clear."

"That's another thing." Mary sat up suddenly under the covers and turned her dark profile to face her. "You need to be careful to always say you have plans."

"Plans?"

"Nanette's the world's worst matchmaker. And I mean *worst* in the worst possible way. If you even hint you're so much as free for an afternoon, she'll set you up. And, um… Let me put it this way. Her setups aren't optimal."

Ventura giggled, unable to imagine the sorts of offerings someone like Nanette might pick out. "I'll take your advice on that too."

"Good." Mary settled back down and rolled toward the wall, wrapping her blanket around her.

Ventura hadn't had a roommate since college, at least not in the same room. She'd shared an apartment with another girl in graduate school, but they'd each had their own space, and Trisha had been so quiet, Ventura had barely ever known she was there. Mary was all the opposite: loud and blustery and all up in Ventura's face. Telling her how to dress and wear her hair, and warning her off Nanette's nutty notions. Ventura had never been close to her big sister, Hope, and had gone through most of her life without having a best friend. She wondered if Mary would become that, even as different from each other as they were.

"Mary," she said quietly before the other girl could drift off to sleep. "Thanks for bringing me here. For letting me know about this apartment."

"I did it for selfish reasons," Mary answered groggily.

"That may be, but you didn't have to take me to the party."

"Shut up and go to sleep."

"Okay."

A few seconds later, she heard Mary's voice. "I'm glad you had fun. You looked like a million bucks."

"Thanks to you."

"Yeah, maybe."

"Do you think I'll ever see him again?"

"Who?"

"Richard."

"Of course you will. Just pick up a paper. He's in it all the time."

She hurled her pillow at Mary with a laugh. "I meant, in person!"

Mary rolled over and clutched it. "My, my. Two days in town and look who's already got a crush."

"I do not," Ventura said, feeling her cheeks warm.

"That's okay. I'll keep your little secret." Mary tossed the pillow back at her. "Let's get some shut-eye. I've got work in the morning, and tomorrow you're cold-calling."

"Right." Ventura snatched back her pillow and pulled it over her head as floorboards moaned above. What an exhausting couple of days she'd had. Once she finally nodded off, she'd no doubt sleep like the dead.

Chapter Three

Richard's personal assistant, Jason, burst through his home office door. As managing editor of his own magazine, Richard had been able to work out a flexible schedule where he telecommuted part of the time from his stylish townhouse in Old Town Alexandria. This helped a great deal when it came to raising the twins. None of the nannies he'd hired to date had been able to function without the highest level of oversight. Jason's face was pink from the neck up as he clutched his tablet to his teal polo shirt. "I've got to talk to you about Helena."

Helena was the latest in a string of caretakers he'd hired to look after Ricky and Elisa. "What's going on?"

"I'm afraid we've had another auto disaster."

Richard spun his chair toward the window framing the street. His new BMW sat there with a bashed-in front hood and sagging bumper. "Not again."

"And the worst part is, she's blaming the—"

"I quit!" Helena said, barreling through the door with her hand-scrawled letter of resignation. She pressed it to Richard's desk and met his gaze with a hostile glare. "Find someone else to look after your little monsters."

Richard bristled and sat up straighter. "Watch yourself."

Jason blinked at Helena, then shared a placating smile. "You *do* want a positive recommendation?"

"Recommendation? Ha!" She huffed and glanced briefly at them both. "Are you kidding? This has been the job from Hades. I'm not even listing it on my résumé." She strode out the door with a cry that made her sound like a wild banshee. They heard a jingle of metal as she grabbed her purse and keys from the hall table; then the front door slammed shut.

Richard sat back in his chair and sighed. He ran a hand through his hair and met Jason's gaze with weary eyes. "What do we do now?"

Jason sat in a chair opposite Richard's desk and began furiously tapping at his tablet. After a few beats, he looked up, fully composed. This was why Richard relied on him. Jason always kept his cool, even under the most dire circumstances. "Advertise."

Ventura woke with a jolt as her pillow was yanked out from under her. "Wake up, sleepyhead! You finally have an interview!"

Ventura squinted up at Mary, who was dressed in a cream-colored skirt and kiwi silk blouse with dangling matching earrings. Ventura hadn't dreamed it. Fashionista Mary had nabbed Ventura's dream job and was working at the *Daily Globe*. She started today. Ventura sat up.

"What time is it?"

"Nearly eight o'clock; I have to get going. So do you. Isn't your appointment at nine?"

"And all the way across town," Ventura wailed. "How could you let me hit snooze?"

Mary set a hand on her hip. "Who I am? Your mother? Besides…" She puckered her lips and put on a dab of Perfectly Plum lipstick. "I was getting ready." She did a little pirouette in her light-colored skirt and matching heels. "What do you think?"

"Like you look too nice to be serving coffee."

"I'll work my way up. You'll see."

Ventura was sure that she would. Mary was pretty and bright and incredibly determined. She'd never even known she'd wanted to work in journalism until she'd considered the fashion angle. There was a whole *section* dedicated to that. Thanks to Ventura's forays into journalism job-hunting, Mary had become greatly inspired. What a wonderful way to influence the world for the better. Just imagine! Mary might someday craft articles that inspired Washingtonians to dress better! It made her tingle all over—just at the thought.

"Have a great first day!" Ventura called as Mary raced up the stairs.

"Thanks!" she shouted back. "Break a leg at the interview!"

Thirty minutes later, Ventura scurried down the front steps and lost a heel. *Great*, she thought, racing back up the stairs to grab it, *I'll never make the Metro on time.* She stepped back into her shoe and her too-tight blouse popped open. Ventura quickly scanned the street for passersby and rebuttoned it with a shake of her head. She should have known better than to borrow this from Mary, but right now it was the most upscale-looking thing she had.

The front door opened, and Nanette stuck her head outside. "Hey, Ventura! When will you be home?"

"I'm not sure," she answered, remembering Mary's warning. Fearing the look in Nanette's eyes, she purposely stretched the truth a bit. "The interviews could take all day."

"All day, but not into the night, eh?" Nanette said with a wink. "Just be sure you're home for dinner. I have a special surprise in store. For you and Mary both!"

That was all she needed, Nanette trying to make her disastrous day *better.*

Ventura hiked up her skirt and ran down the street, her damp hair flying behind her. She hadn't had time to dry it, much less press it flat with that torture implement Mary called the *Magic Wand of Fashion.* She was halfway down the escalator when she heard a light *rip.* Ventura glanced down in horror to see her hose had run right at mid-thigh. Well maybe her skirt would cover it. If not, she'd primly cross her legs. *What a mother of a day this is turning out to be*, Ventura thought, springing into the silver Metro car seconds before metal doors closed.

Ventura gripped the handrail, studying the Metro map plastered on the wall and catching her breath. She thought she was supposed to take the Blue Line. But maybe she'd made the wrong connection at Metro Center. What if she was headed to Northern Virginia when her interview was downtown?

"Need help?"

Ventura turned her attention from the map on the wall toward his voice, encountering that incredibly handsome face. "Richard!" she cried, scarcely able to believe it. Here she stood, looking perfectly horrible, and his gorgeous brown eyes were gazing at her.

He grinned, apparently pleased by her recognition. "I'm surprised that you remember." As if in a million years she could forget. "We met at the gala a few weeks ago. It's Ventura, isn't it?"

She nodded numbly, wanting to sink through the subway car's floor. How he'd positively identified her based on how she'd looked before and the way she did now, she had no idea.

"You look different."

She sucked in a breath, wanting to die.

"Have you changed your hair?"

"It's, um…" She nervously flipped wet tresses back over her shoulder. "Just not dry yet."

He appraised her with a nod. "Well, I like it this way. Very natural."

"Oh."

"So many people in this city are into pretense. Overdoing everything, when sometimes it's best to just let things be."

"Yes."

"So, where are you headed?"

"I have an interview on K Street."

"Which end?"

"I have the address right… Hang on a second." She fumbled in her purse for her billfold, then pulled it out and flipped it open. She'd written the particulars on a Post-it note, which she'd tucked in the flap for cash. She pulled it out and handed it over. To her dismay, she saw something else had stuck to its gummy back.

Richard studied the address, then, feeling something on the back of the Post-it, turned it over and read the message on her secret fortune. Ventura winced.

His face warmed all over. "I keep a four-leaf clover in my pocket, you know."

"You do not," she said, barely breathing the words.

He shrugged noncommittally. "Suit yourself."

Ventura reached over and pulled the white slip of paper off the Post-it, then jammed it back in her wallet. "I have no idea how that got there," she said with a little laugh. "Could have been there for ages."

"Really?"

Subway bells chimed, and the doors slid open as new groups of passengers boarded and disembarked, but Ventura felt unable to move a muscle. She just stood there, caught up in his gorgeous dark eyes.

Richard stepped a few inches closer, and Ventura's heart hammered harder. "Ventura," he said as the doors clipped shut, "I think that was your stop."

Lucky for her, Richard took pity on her plight and offered to escort her to Farragut North. They stood saying their good-byes outside the station, in the small park adjoining the square. An azure sky opened up above them while pigeons fluttered all around.

"I hope your interview goes well."

"Thanks for getting me here. I never would have made it alone."

"You'll get the hang of things quickly enough."

"I hope so."

He studied her a moment, considering something. "I wish I could offer you a spot at the magazine, but we've got a really small shop."

"It's all right, I understand."

He nodded and pulled a business card from his jacket. "Say Ventura… You wouldn't consider…? I mean, I know it might seem out of line for me to suggest…"

Ventura's pulse picked up a notch as she met his gaze. Was he about to ask her to lunch? Maybe even out for dinner?"

"But I do have an opening at home."

"Home?"

"Help watching my kids." His handsome face registered concern. "We had some trouble with our last nanny."

Ventura's world caved in on her. Naturally, she should have known. There she'd been thinking that

Richard was flirting with her, angling to ask her on a date. When all he'd wanted in truth was domestic assistance.

"I'm afraid I'm not in the nanny business."

"But you do have experience? With children, I mean?"

"Well, of course, I babysat in high school. A little bit in college too." Ventura stopped herself. Where was this going? She didn't need to provide explanations to this man. She was here to work in journalism and had spent a lot of time going to school for it besides. "I appreciate the thought," she finally said. "But I'm really looking for something different."

"Of course you are," he said with kind understanding, but he handed her his card just the same. "I hope you'll take this anyway. Just in case."

"Just in case?"

"You come across someone who might be qualified?" He raised his brow with a hopeful expression. "You can have them reach me here."

Mary widened her eyes at Ventura, then glanced toward the kitchen. "I think we should serve dessert." They sat in the dining room with two of Nanette's late-day surprises. Even in her scariest dreams, Ventura couldn't have imagined anything this bad.

Ventura plucked Larry's clammy grip from her knee. "Sounds like a plan."

"Don't be in such a hurry, darlin'," Larry purred. Ventura pushed back in her chair, its legs loudly scraping the wooden floorboards beneath it. He was impossibly thin and *old*. For sure pushing fifty, with a balding head and bulging eyes that were charcoal in color like his pilled sweater vest.

Ventura cleared their plates and scurried toward the kitchen, fighting the urge to retch.

"Wait for me!" Mary yelped, clanking silverware together as she nabbed things off the table and hurried after her. But not quickly enough. Potbellied Louis leaned back in his chair to pinch her butt with a chortle when she passed by, muttering something about bringing him plenty of sugar.

"You boys are so bad!" Nanette said, slapping her end of the table with a giggle. "Next time, you'll have to bring a friend for me."

Mary passed through the swinging kitchen door with a gasp. "What did I tell you?"

Ventura dumped her dishes in the sink in disbelief. "Those guys are at least twice our age."

"Politicians think they can get away with it."

"Yuck!"

"No joke."

Ventura heaved a sigh and leaned back against the counter. "What was Nanette thinking?"

"Maybe they looked good to *her*." Mary shrugged. "Her judgement's not all that, you know."

"I wish we'd had some warning."

"Nanette's sneaky that way. Though she'll usually drop a hint." Mary suspiciously eyed Ventura. "Did she say anything to you? Anything at all?"

"She might have made some mild suggestion on my way out the door this morning." Ventura grimaced. "But honestly, I had no idea."

"No, of course you didn't."

"I'm sorry this had to happen to you on your first day of your new job. How did it go?"

"I burned the coffee."

"I'm sure they'll forgive you."

"Four times."

"But I thought you'd worked at a coffee shop?"

"Serving, not cooking."

"Well, I missed my Metro stop."

"You what?"

She smiled mysteriously. "That didn't mean I couldn't find a Washington hottie to help me."

"Ventura! What are you talking about? You met someone?"

"I saw Richard," Ventura whispered. "And, oh my goodness, Mary, I looked a total wreck."

Mary paused a beat to study her. "You don't look bad now."

"It was worse in the morning with run pantyhose and wild wet hair."

Mary cupped her mouth with her hand. "Are you serious?"

"Naturally, Richard was as put together as always."

"He's impeccable, that one is. I want the name of his tailor."

Ventura produced Richard's business card. "Well, you can call him and ask."

Mary's expression brightened. "Nice work. He gave you his card? What's up?"

Ventura felt her face fall at the admission. "He wants a nanny."

"That's it?"

"Oh, girls!" Nanette hollered from the next room. "Your gentlemen friends are growing restless!"

Mary opened her mouth and stuck in a finger, making a gagging motion.

Ventura giggled before growing serious again. "What are we going to do?"

"We've got to get rid of them."

"The sooner the better. But how?"

Mary pursed her lips in thought, then pulled a carton of ice cream from the freezer with an evil grin. "Men a la mode?" she whispered to Ventura. And then, much more loudly, she called to Nanette, "Coming right up!"

A few minutes later, Ventura primly carted in dessert plates loaded with generous slices of pecan pie. Mary followed with a container of ice cream and a solid silver scoop.

Larry eyed Ventura lasciviously as she set down his plate. "Why, thanks, sweetness."

Mary coquettishly batted her eyelashes. "Ice cream with that?"

Larry licked his lips, and Ventura shuddered. "Tasty-tasty."

With incredible cool, Mary dug a huge mound of ice cream out of the box then… "Whoops! Oh, heavens to Betsy!" she proclaimed, putting on an exaggerated Southern tone. "Just what have I done?"

"Hey!" Larry spewed, springing from his chair as the cold ball of French Vanilla landed square in his lap.

Ventura set down Louis's dessert with a smile. "How about you?"

"I'm sure he wants some too," Mary went on without skipping a beat. Before Louis could get another word out, she'd scooped out two more hunks of ice cream and "Uh-oh!"

"Oh dear." Ventura brought her hands to her cheeks, surveying the double balls nestled together above Louis's plaid pants.

He pushed back in his chair with a scowl, sweeping the ice cream balls off his lap and onto the Oriental carpet under the table.

"My good rug!" Nanette cried with dismay.

Louis stood haughtily, joining Larry by the door in the foyer.

"I don't think that was any kind of accident," Larry scolded, still dabbing his slacks with his hanky.

Nanette stood from her chair, clearly offended. "Now, I'm sure they didn't do that on purpose."

"Of course not," Mary said before Ventura added, "We're so sorry."

"Harrumph!" Larry leaned forward to wipe Louis's crotch, and Louis slapped him. "Stop that! We're in public now!"

The girls raised their brows at each other.

"Why don't we all sit back down—" Nanette began.

"Not on your life, sister." Louis already had his hand on the knob and was pulling the front door open.

A few minutes later, the three women leaned out the door and watched the men scamper down the sidewalk, their knees bent out sideways like bow-legged cowboys.

"Don't forget to call!" Nanette yelled after them, which only made them move faster.

Chapter Four

Jason smiled politely at the preppy blonde in pearls as he walked her to the door. "Thanks so much for stopping by. We'll get back to you by the end of the week."

After seeing her outside, he returned to Richard, who sat with his elbows on his desk, head in hands. "None of them are any good."

"I didn't think Helga was so horrible."

Richard set his palms on his desk and stared at him. "She was scary. Admit it."

"Okay. Just a tiny bit. But Ricky and Elisa need discipline. You said so yourself."

"Not *that* kind. The woman didn't even smile."

"So maybe she has dental problems?"

"You're not helping her case."

Jason sat heavily in a chair. "Guess I'm not." He flipped back through his tablet and shook his head. "Looks like we've gone through all of them."

"Maybe we need to up what we're paying?" Richard suggested.

"We're already paying double the going rate."

"I don't want just anyone looking after my kids."

"Of course you don't."

"She has to be smart."

"Naturally."

"Attentive."

"Goes without saying."

"Nimble enough to think on her feet."

"And in the car."

Richard spouted a laugh. "Too true." He smiled at Jason, grateful to have him in his company, not just as an assistant but as a friend. He'd been asking too much of him these past few weeks, having him pick up some nanny duties in addition to his already demanding job. Richard had to find a solution to this and soon. "Any brilliant thoughts?"

"We can call some of the local colleges. A few have babysitting lists."

"I don't know how the scheduling would work for somebody taking classes, but I guess we could give that a whirl."

"I'll get on it right away."

"Thanks, Jason."

Jason met his eyes with a compassionate gaze. "Don't worry, chief. We'll find someone. And once we do, I'm going to guarantee it, she'll have been worth the wait."

Ventura stared down at Richard's business card in a sweat. For three weeks, she'd been pounding the pavement, cold-calling, and applying online, and so far she'd had only two meager interviews, neither of which had panned out. It was impossible to believe that with a graduate degree she couldn't even land a secretarial job, but in this competitive market, that was how it seemed. And now, she was running out of money.

She pulled a tissue from the box on the table to dab her damp forehead and too-hot neck. Since theirs was a basement apartment, Nanette didn't believe air-conditioning was warranted. But by mid-June in Washington, even basement apartments were broiling hot. Not that Ventura blamed Nanette for pinching pennies. She basically lived on a widow's pension supplemented by her meager rental income. Though this place was stretching her thin, it was far less expensive than any other place Ventura might rent on her own. And what she'd lost in privacy, she'd gained in a special new friend. It seemed she and Mary became closer every day. If only Ventura were gainfully employed, she'd feel better about things. As it was, she was having to be extra careful about finances.

She'd tried to gloss over it, but Mary appeared to have picked up on it just the same. Just last night she'd offered to pay their tab for Zen's Chinese Take-Out, supposedly in celebration of receiving her first big paycheck. Inwardly, Ventura knew Mary was being kind. Ventura was getting to the point where she could no longer afford take-out food. Things were getting desperate. If there were another way, she'd seize it. But the only other way Ventura could see at the moment involved giving up on her dreams entirely and moving back home. And home wasn't a place where Ventura was necessarily welcome. Her mom had sold the big house and moved into a condo, which basically accommodated her and her half-time, live-in boyfriend, along with his gigantic, drool-happy dog.

Ventura took a long sip of water, then set down the bottle, preparing to dial. She hoped to find a way to sound casual about it and not present herself as being quite as desperate as she was. She couldn't chance giving Richard the idea that there was something wrong with her. She'd at least need to secure an interview to have a shot at the job. She punched in Richard's number and fidgeted nervously with her scrawled-on legal pad as the phone rang two, then three times… In case he didn't answer, she'd written down precisely what she would say to his voice-mail box.

"Richard Blake," he answered in an even clip that sounded ultraprofessional.

Ventura stared hard at her legal pad, and all sense of reason flew out the window. "Um…"

"Is someone there?" he asked seriously.

"Yes! Hello. This is Ventura Hart."

He paused a beat, then answered, "Ventura, hi. How nice to hear from you. How's the job hunt going?"

"Not so well," she answered honestly.

"I'm"—he hesitated a moment before finishing—"sorry."

"Yes, well. You know how it is."

"Very competitive market."

"Exactly."

"Not that you're not extremely qualified."

"Thanks."

"I've been asking around."

"You have?"

"The only problem is, I didn't have a way to contact you."

Ventura drew a hopeful breath. "You mean, you've heard of something? In journalism?"

"No," he said quickly. "Not exactly. But I've been keeping my ears open."

"That's good of you."

"Yes."

"Well, you have my number now."

"It's on my caller ID," he agreed.

"Which may come in handy."

"How so?"

"Should"—Ventura gathered her nerve and squeezed shut her eyes—"you need to call me for interview?"

"Interview?"

Ventura drew a breath and let it out, counting to twenty-five.

"Ventura? Are you still there?"

"I'd like to apply for the position," she told him firmly.

"The nanny job?" he asked with surprise.

"If you'll still have me."

"It's yours!" he proclaimed with delight.

"Whhh…what did you say?"

"I said, you're hired, Ventura. When can you start?"

"But don't I need to interview? Meet the kids?"

"Formalities. We'll arrange all that. Doesn't have to be in any certain order."

"I see." Ventura swallowed hard, wondering what she was getting herself into. How bad were those children if he hadn't found help for them already? Ventura tried to reassure herself, thinking Richard was probably just picky as any good daddy would be. That made him admirable, didn't it?

"It would super if you could swing by on Monday. You can meet the kids and Jason, and we'll get everything set up."

"Jason?"

"He's my personal assistant and a really great guy. You'll have no worries. Jason will teach you everything you need to learn in getting started. Now, all I need is your address. I'll have him come and pick you up."

Ventura set down her cell in a daze as Mary entered the kitchen.

"What's up?" Mary asked her. "You look a little weird."

"I've just been hired."

"That's awesome!" Mary walked over and slapped her a high-five. "Where?"

"At Richard's."

"You took the nanny job?"

Ventura nodded, still dumbstruck. It had all happened so fast she could scarcely believe it herself.

"When do you start?"

"On Monday."

"That's great! We'll have to celebrate."

"Did I hear someone say celebrate?" Nanette asked, tottering down the stairs in platform sandals.

Ventura and Mary shared frightened looks.

"What a wonderful coincidence that is! My cousin Frank has a nice young nephew in town." Ventura's mouth hung open as Mary grimaced, seconds before Nanette appeared in a poodle skirt and tiny tank top. "He and his friend Charles are Capitol Hill interns. Imagine that. We're practically neighbors."

"Imagine," Mary said, blinking at Ventura.

"Trying not to," Ventura said under her breath.

Nanette studied them both with an affectionate grin. "Naturally, I told Frank you'd show the boys around."

Cherry trees and dogwoods lined the Tidal Basin reflecting the Jefferson Memorial as the sun rose high above the water. Ventura and Mary shared a paddleboat as two toned blonds, Charles and Wally, commandeered another. The guys smiled and waved, tipping their visors in the girls' direction.

Ventura stared at them in awe. "I have to hand it to Nanette. This time, she didn't mess up."

"I know. Amazing. Right?" Mary grinned and waved back. "Which one do you like best?"

"They're both really cute."

"You choose."

Just then, Ventura spotted a hunky, dark-haired man strolling along the path with two gorgeous children in tow, a boy and a girl who both looked to be about five years old. The man moved with confidence and the easy grace of a guy in charge of himself, not to mention his rock-hard body. "I'll take him," she said a bit wistfully.

Mary gripped her arm and whispered, "Oh my gosh, Ventura. It's *him.*"

"Who?"

"Richard!"

Ventura lowered her prescription sunglasses to get a clearer view, seeing Mary was right. It was Richard, no doubt, dressed in khaki slacks and a crisp white polo, buying his two adorable children ice cream from a kiosk vendor.

"You've got it made in the shade working for that dude."

"Can't beat the view," Ventura said with a sigh.

"Do you think he sees us?"

"No, and let's keep it that way. When I meet his kids on Monday, I want to present myself professionally."

As they spoke, Wally and Charles drew their boat up beside them. "You girls about ready for our picnic?"

Ventura scanned the shore to spy Richard and his kids nowhere in sight. "Sounds fine."

"I'm starved," Mary agreed.

Charles gave Ventura a warm smile. "Great. Let's head back to the dock, then, and throw a blanket down somewhere."

"So much for *our* choosing," Mary said as they turned their boat around.

"What do you mean?" Ventura asked her.

"I think Charles has a thing for you."

"Really?" Ventura asked, fingering her flat-ironed hair.

"You do look dynamite in those short shorts."

Ventura studied her thighs and the way they pudged out sideways on the seat of the boat. "They might be a bit too short."

"No way! You, girlfriend, look smoking hot. And don't think someone hasn't noticed," she said, angling her chin at the boat up ahead as Charles kept trying to sneak peeks at Ventura over his shoulder.

Before she knew it, they were back at the dock and the boys had already disembarked. "Here," Charles said to Ventura, playing the gentleman, "give me your hand."

Ventura stood unsteadily as the small craft rocked. Taking his hand was probably a good idea. It was going to be a little tricky climbing out of here, especially in these thigh-high shorts and with—-*what?*—Richard walking right toward her! Ventura made a sudden shift, and her wet sneaker squeaked on the boat's bottom.

"Ventura!" Charles urged, extending his arm "Here!"

But all she could see was Richard, with his unbelievably dark eyes and incredibly sexy smile, striding in her direction. She reached for Charles's hand but missed it just as Richard's surprised gaze settled on hers.

"Ventura!" he called, rushing forth as she stepped off the boat and sank like a stone in the water. In the split second before her life vest bobbed her back up, Ventura's whole life flashed before her.

She felt herself spiraling down…down into the cold, her hair swirling around her like strings of seaweed. This was it—her life's most embarrassing moment, and she was going to die from it besides. Get sucked right down into the murky depths of the Tidal Basin where she could meet the ghosts of her great political forefathers: Jefferson, Lincoln, Kennedy… Who else was memorialized around here? Hang on one second! It wasn't about to be her! She held her breath and stretched up her arms, kicking and flailing her way to the surface as her life vest lifted her heavenward. She was nearly there when two strong hands grabbed her wrists and pulled her into the light. Ventura gasped for air, sucking in a deep breath.

"Are you all right?"

She looked up at the man holding on to her as the others crowded in with worried faces.

"I…think so," she said with a cough.

Richard heaved a sigh of relief and smiled down at her. "Let me help you out of there."

He bent low to assist her as Ventura pressed her hands to the dock and hoisted herself out of the water. Ventura crossed her arms in front of her chest and stood there dripping. Her hair was a tangled mess, and her sunglasses dangled from where they'd been caught up in her necklace.

"Thank you," she told Richard as his two children stared at her agape.

"Do you *know* her?" the boy asked his dad with undisguised horror.

"Ricky, Elisa," Richard said, grinning broadly. "I'd like you to meet Ventura, your new nanny."

Little Elisa threw her head back with a wail that could be heard for miles around. "*Noooooo!*"

Chapter Five

The following Monday morning, Jason drove Ventura past the US Capitol building and toward the Washington Monument, before crossing the bridge that would lead them to Old Town Alexandria. The glistening waters of the Potomac sparkled below as sailboats with colorful spinnakers drifted by. An occasional motorboat tore across the waves, revving its engine and kicking up a wake.

"Richard wanted me to apologize for the way his kids behaved on Saturday," Jason offered with a genial sideways glance.

"I'm sure I was a shock to them."

"Still, they went a little overboard." Such a PR man. Ventura wondered what Richard paid him but ventured it had to be in the high five figures. "I haven't heard of them behaving that way for a couple of nannies now."

"A couple?" Ventura asked in shock. "How many have there been?"

Jason set his jaw and peered through the windshield. "Oh, six… No, seven."

"Oh!"

"Since January, I mean." He turned briefly to face her, then set his eyes back on the road. "Altogether there've been fifteen."

"Fifteen?" Ventura swallowed hard. "And how old are the children?"

"The twins just turned five."

Ventura divided quickly, figuring that was an average of three nannies a year! And math wasn't even her strength.

"Don't worry," Jason said, seeming to read her mind. "It's not nearly as bad as you think. Richard's only been on his own for three years."

They drove down cobblestone streets, passing crowds of shoppers and a guitar-strumming street musician huddled up against a curio shop. Before long, Jason steered the car into a narrow parallel parking spot before a quaint white-bricked townhome, complete with flowering window boxes and a wrought iron front gate.

Two children bounded out the door as Ventura cautiously exited the car.

"Ventura!" little Ricky said, racing toward her. "You came!"

Elisa shot her a shy grin and raced after her brother.

Maybe this wasn't going to be as bad as she'd thought. Kids were kids, after all. And these were mighty cute ones.

Ricky threw his arms around her with a hug. Ventura stooped low to embrace him, and he sweetly patted her head. "We're so glad you're here."

Elisa silently stood by and nodded.

"Why, thanks, Ricky." She hugged him back, puzzled at the rapid turn of events. Perhaps Richard had talked to them and warned them to mind their manners.

"Ventura," Richard said, emerging from the door. "You made it."

She straightened her spine and smoothed her hair, which was as silky as satin by now. While she opted to wear it curly most days, she now employed a deep conditioner that gave her soft ringlets instead of frizz. She was also getting used to wearing her contacts and had decided Mary was right. She did look better without the glasses. More importantly, she felt better too. Ventura didn't know when it was that she'd completely given up on her appearance. Though perhaps it was more accurate to say, she'd never paid that much attention to it. Now that she was starting to, things seemed to be coming together for her. It was like she was developing confidence in herself as a woman for the very first time.

"It was a nice drive," Ventura said, flipping back her hair. She twitched suddenly, sensing something was amiss. Why did the top of her head itch like something was on it? She raised her hand to her crown, then squealed in horror. "What *is* it?" she yelped as Ricky and Elisa giggled, scampering away. She thrust her fingers into her hair and encountered a tiny solid object. *Please,* she prayed plucking it free, *don't let it be alive.* And when she examined it in the sunlight, she saw that it wasn't. It was merely a little plastic spider, the kind used to decorate cupcakes at Halloween.

"The kids must like you," Richard told her. "With the others, the spiders were real."

When they entered the house, Ricky ran through the hall chasing Elisa, who held a squishy, bug-eyed toad. "Blinkie! She's got my Blinkie!" Ricky cried with dismay.

"Elisa! Ricky!" Richard warned. The kids skittered across polished hardwood floors, then tore up the steps. "Slow down! Somebody's going to get hurt!"

Ventura turned to Jason. "I don't suppose it's a plastic frog?"

Just then, Elisa catapulted something from the top of the stairs. She'd raced up them, taking them two at a time, paces ahead of Ricky and her father.

Ventura stared down in horror as something landed at her feet with a *sprong!* The life-like toad split open, exposing electronic inner workings, tiny springs, and torn wires.

"Looks like another trip to the cyber-pet shop," Jason quipped.

He disappeared for a moment, then returned with a broom and dustpan. "Your first clean-up mission," Jason said, handing it to Ventura. She looked down at the mess before her, her stomach churning at the thought she'd imagined this thing to be real.

"I need to talk to the kids," Richard said, excusing himself.

Two hours later, Richard sat at his large modern desk. A new cyber toad croaked and bounced about in its cage beside his laptop computer. None of her studies had prepared Ventura for a day this wild. The house was a maze, the kids were a mess, and expectations for the nanny were exponential. Richard handed over two hefty day-planners and Ventura squirmed in her chair.

"The yellow one's Elisa's. Purple is for Ricky."

Ventura stared at him astounded. "These are their schedules?"

"Hard copies. Naturally, we've got e-files. I'll have Jason upload them to your smart phone."

"Um."

"You do have a smart phone?"

Ventura reached in her purse and extracted her antiquated cell, the kind that came with the most basic plan. And that was six years ago.

"No worries." Richard shot her a soothing smile, and Ventura's heart stilled. How she wished he wouldn't do that. Smile at her in that super hot way that made her wish they were out on a date rather than discussing her business duties. Ventura bit her bottom lip, hoping that thought hadn't been written all over her face. But maybe it had been. Because at this very moment, Richard had stopped talking and was gazing intently into her eyes. She wondered if he sensed it too, this secret pull between them. Or perhaps it wasn't mutual at all, and there was no pull—only her overworked imagination futilely tugging.

Richard seemed to snap himself out of it, picking up on his earlier thought. "We'll work all that out. You'll definitely need high-tech communication to be part of our team." Ventura thought of her decrepit old laptop but didn't mention it. "I'll get Jason to set you up with a new phone tomorrow."

"You mean like a company phone?" she queried.

"You can keep it for personal use as well. We'll cover the charges as long as you're employed."

"Thanks, that's very nice." She looked down at the huge day-planners in her lap, then opened the purple one on top. An enormous spreadsheet accordianed out of its front pocket. "Wow."

"Kids need structure," Richard assured her. "Keeps them busy."

"Very," Ventura said, unable to stop herself, as she opened Elisa's folder and another enormous spreadsheet tumbled out.

Richard cleared his throat. "You're not suggesting the kids are overscheduled?"

"Not at all," she said quickly. "It's just that…" She studied Elisa's list. "Ballet… Piano… Soccer… Karate…? How old is Elisa again?"

"Five. Oh, I know!" he said, apparently misreading her look. "She should really be a brown belt by now. I had no clue I was supposed to start her in PeeWee K at age three."

Ventura gulped. She had no doubt that Richard loved his children, but it appeared they scarcely had any time to be kids.

His handsome face took on a touch of melancholy. "Vicky used to handle everything," he confided. "If it hadn't been for Jason, I never would have been able to keep things together."

Her heart ached for him. It was hard to imagine what that might have been like, being left on his own with two little babies. So maybe he *did* overschedule them, but was that really his fault? Richard was simply being a good dad in the only way he knew how—by being super organized. "I'm sorry, Richard," she said sincerely. "That sounds rough."

He met her gaze with soulful eyes. "At times, it has been."

She wasn't sure what else to say. Suddenly things between them seemed to have gone from professional to personal. But maybe that's how it was going to be. It would be difficult not to develop some kind of personal relationship with Richard if they were both working in the interest of the same thing—the benefit of his children.

"In any case," he said after a beat, "the system we've put together seems to work reasonably well. Jason's a master at scheduling. Even coordinated both kids' activities in a way to minimize driving time."

Ventura's heart skipped a beat. "Maybe I should have told you. I don't own a car."

"Wouldn't expect you to drive your own," he said, nabbing a set of keys off the holder on his desk.

Ventura stared out the front window. The shiny blue convertible Jason had picked her up in sat at the curb. "I'm not sure I should drive that."

Richard laughed. "That one's not suited to car seats. You'll take the Lexus." He handed over the keychain, and their palms brushed. It was just the slightest touch, but Ventura felt electrified by it just the same. Richard held her gaze, reddening slightly at the temples. "You are a good driver? No accidents?"

"Not even a parking ticket."

"Great, because this baby's brand new. We wouldn't want history repeating itself."

"What happened to the last one?"

"The nanny totaled it."

There was a loud pounding from upstairs in the hall and then the rising sound of Jason's voice, "Hey, kids! I said open up!"

"Uh-oh." Richard rose from his chair. "I'd better go investigate."

Ventura eyed the cage on his desk. "Another frog?"

He strode quickly from the room. "Another clog's more like it."

Richard and Ventura arrived in the upstairs hall just as Jason prepared to thrust his shoulder into the bathroom door. "Stand back!" he warned the kids. "I'm coming through on three! One... Two... Oomph!" He threw his weight into the door, and it swung open, ricocheting against the claw-foot tub.

At the opposite end of the room, Ricky and Elisa stood on either side of the commode, their little mouths dropped open. Toilet paper littered the floor along with empty shampoo bottles, several empty cracker boxes and—Ventura could scarcely believe it—an open jar of peanut butter! Elisa stood her with her arms frozen over the toilet in midair, her hands clutching an upside-down potato chip bag. Ricky, who'd been squirting whipped cream around the rim of the bowl, held the can straight out in front of him and pointed it in their direction.

"Ricky!" Richard commanded. "Put that thing down!"

"Now, Elisa!" Ricky urged his sister. "Flush it! Flush it fast!"

Ventura's eyes traveled to the gold-plated toilet paper holder, seeing sheets from the roll had been pulled long—and deposited in the toilet with everything else.

"Don't do it," Richard grated between clenched teeth.

Elisa laid one finger on the handle and met Ventura square in the eye.

"Elisa, no!" Jason called.

Without a hint of emotion, she flushed, sending the rest of the toilet paper on the holder spiraling into the already overloaded bowl. The commode gurgled to life, then erupted in a wild spray that momentarily blinded Richard. Jason beat back the stream with his hands and fell to his knees, wrestling with the water valve on the wall. The kids wailed, apparently terrified by their own horrific doings. Little Ricky blubbered as filthy water repeatedly lapped at his face, while Elisa screamed and shook her soaking hair as tears streamed from her eyes. Ventura lunged forward to pull the kids out of the fray, but her shoe caught on a slick piece of paper. "Ahhh!" she cried, stumbling forward and barely breaking her fall by clutching the toilet's rim. But it was too late— gravity had already taken hold, and her face was set on a downward trajectory—straight into the center of the nasty bowl.

Richard sat in the front seat of his car beside Ventura in awkward silence as he drove her back across the Potomac. He'd been so mortified by the bathroom fiasco, he must have apologized for his children a hundred times. Ventura hadn't said much since she'd pulled her head out of that murky mess and he'd handed her that face towel. He hoped she wasn't planning to sue, but wouldn't necessarily blame her for having those thoughts. He didn't know why his little angels morphed into devils half of the time, but they certainly appeared to have a wild streak. Richard had long wondered if it was because they'd missed a mother's touch.

At first, he thought having a nanny around might help fix that. Of course, it wouldn't be nearly as nice for them as having a real mom, but the right sort of nanny might provide a suitable substitute. But finding the perfect caretaker for Ricky and Elisa had proved more difficult than Richard had imagined. Even the fairly good ones had possessed some kind of quirk, like Jasmine, who'd been great in every way apart from her penchant for listening to rap music. He'd only learned about it by accident when little Elisa and Ricky began spouting ghetto talk peppered with four-letter words. That was the trouble with nannies. You had to trust them implicitly and believe that their judgment was sound, even when it came to picking out radio stations around the five-year-old twins.

Richard glanced at Ventura with her wild wet hair, still flecked by tiny pieces of toilet paper, knowing she'd never make that kind of mistake. Ventura was bright and had a good head on her shoulders. She was educated and articulate too. She would make a fabulous role model for the kids and appeared to be really even tempered. Any of his previous nannies would have gone ballistic over the bathroom escapade, but Ventura had merely turned beet red yet kept her cool. She hadn't once raised her voice or said a negative word against the children. She'd just accepted that towel from him, wiped her face, and dabbed her hair, saying something about that being quite an introduction to Old Town plumbing. Ventura had a calm way about her and a great sense of humor. She was perfect in every way. The sad thing was, after today, he was sure she wouldn't stay. Richard pulled up to the curb beside her Capitol Hill townhouse, feeling down. This was it. Another nanny was about to quit.

"Ventura," he told her quietly. "I want you to know you'll still get your full month's pay."

She shot him a pained look. "You're firing me?"

"Firing you?" Richard stumbled on the words. "Not at all." Then the clarity of her words hit him. He turned to her, stunned. "You mean, you don't quit?"

"Quit?" Her cheeks colored sweetly. "I was just getting my feet wet." She smiled wryly and flipped back her hair. "And other things too, apparently."

Richard laughed with relief, unable to believe her. How could she be so incredibly good-natured in the face of such calamity? "Ventura," he said with a sigh. "You don't know how happy I am to hear you say that."

"I'm sure it was a freak thing," she told him. "Surely, every day won't be that bad."

Richard pursed his lips and tried not to recall the string of disasters that had befallen the other nannies. Clearly, none of that would happen to Ventura. She was better than that. Primed for the challenge. Just look at her sitting there with whipped cream behind her ear, oblivious to how ridiculously cute she looked. Richard swallowed hard, stopping himself. He was not supposed to be thinking about "cute" and "nanny" together. If he wanted Ventura to stay on, theirs would need to be a professional relationship. Richard was sure that wouldn't be hard at all. There'd never been any lines crossed with any of the other girls. He hadn't even entertained the thought. Come to think of it, Richard hadn't really entertained the thought of becoming involved with any woman in quite some time. And that was just how he would keep things. "I'm sure you're right," he told her with growing confidence. "Tomorrow's bound to be better."

"What monsters!" Mary proclaimed. People stared in their direction, and she lowered her voice. "I can't believe they did all that in one day."

They stood in line at Zen's Chinese Take-Out. Ventura had been so unnerved, she hadn't even wanted to shower first. Nothing could calm her nerves like an order of pork fried rice. "I know," Ventura answered. "If I'd been watching it instead of living it, it might even have seemed funny."

"Ha-ha," Mary deadpanned. "Bet you're laughing all the way to the bank."

"What do you mean?" Ventura asked as the line inched forward.

"Come on, Richard's got ca-ching. Loads of it, from what I hear. So why not crank it up a notch and ask for a raise?"

"A raise?" Ventura hadn't even considered it. She was just grateful she still had a job. As bad as it seemed, first days were bound to be rocky. Truth was, things could only go up from there. "I don't know, Mary. I don't want to push it."

"Push what? The guy's lucky you're not pressing charges!"

"Against two five-year-olds?" Ventura asked in shock.

"Well, yeah. Okay. I kind of see your point."

Ventura felt a tap on her shoulder and turned with a start to see—*oh no, not today*—Charles! He flashed each of them a pleasant grin. "I thought I saw you girls talking up here."

"Hey! No butting in line!" an angry woman called.

Charles nodded deferentially. "Just passing through," he told the woman, who watched him with an eagle eye just the same.

Charles met Ventura's gaze. "I've been thinking about you. Thinking of calling."

She self-consciously fingered her hair, her nail catching on a dried piece of toilet paper. "Really?"

"Our first date ended so badly."

"Through no fault of yours," she added hastily.

"Accidents happen." He tilted his head to the side. "Did you change your hair?"

"Order up!" the cook called from the front.

The woman behind them loudly cleared her throat.

"Five more seconds," Charles told her, before turning his attention back to Ventura. "In any case, I was thinking we might try it again. This time, away from the water?"

Ventura laughed lightly, thinking what a good guy he was. What harm would it be? One little date? Ventura didn't have many friends in Washington. It never hurt to make more. "I'd like that."

Charles shot her a big, bold grin. "That's great. Just great! I'll call you." Then he strode to the back of the line before the disgruntled older woman could shoot daggers in his back with her eyes.

Chapter Six

The next morning, Mary opened the door to Nanette's townhouse to find an incredibly dapper guy standing outside. His pale pink button-down was pressed, light starch, and his navy slacks were pleated to a tee. Even his boat shoes looked brand-new.

"Um… I'm here for Ventura?"

Mary met bright blue eyes, and her heart beat faster. Who was this fashion god, and why hadn't he come calling sooner? Hang on! For Ventura? For a gal in constant need of a makeover, she certainly seemed to be having all the luck.

"I'm Jason," he said, extending a hand. "Richard's personal assistant." Of course he was. How else would one explain Richard's impeccable wardrobe and the high-class way he dressed his children? He had a built-in fashion consultant.

"Coming, Jason!" Ventura called, nearly stumbling up the basement stairs. She dropped her purse to the floor and a roll of mints spilled out, spiraling toward Jason's shoe. He bent low to pick it up, and Mary gasped with delight. That was no fifteen-dollar haircut, she thought, studying the perfectly tapered lines of his short blond hair. *This* was high couture!

Mary's face pinched as she wiggled her nose at an itch.

It was only then that she remembered she wore her damp hair in a towel turban-style and that she had a *Salt of the Earth* mud mask drying on her face! Jason stepped aside and Ventura scurried out the door, then met Mary's gaze with a smile. "Nice meeting you…?"

She blinked twice, hoping this was all some horrid dream and that it would poof away. But it didn't. He just stood there, waiting for her to give him her name.

"Mary," she filled in with a squeak.

A few seconds later, Ventura sat behind the wheel of the huge SUV. When Richard said she'd be driving the Lexus, she'd envisioned a sedan, not something this enormous.

Jason glanced back toward the house. "Mary seems nice."

"She's a great roommate," Ventura assured him. "She's probably really embarrassed you saw her that way."

"Why's that?"

"You don't know, Mary. She's always gorgeously dressed. Perfectly put together from head to toe."

Jason raised his brow, intrigued. "Really?"

Ventura fumbled with the keys in the ignition.

"Just go ahead and get it started. We're going to run a few practice rounds before heading back to the ranch."

"Practice rounds?"

"Richard thought it would be good for you to get the feel of the SUV before driving with the kids on board."

She nodded and cranked the engine with trembling fingers. "Where to?"

"We can take a few spins around the block, then maybe head down to the Mall."

Ventura swallowed hard, knowing the area that housed the Smithsonian museums was always jam-packed with tourists. Pedestrian tourists. Especially in summertime.

"But first," he said with a smile, "we're going to have to get out of this parallel parking spot."

Sweat beaded on Ventura's forehead as she attempted to maneuver the beast of a vehicle for what seemed like the hundredth time. She'd inched back and forth, and back and forth...but didn't seem be getting anywhere nearer to extracting them from this tight space between the minivan up ahead and the tiny red sports car behind them.

Jason checked his cell for the time, comparing it to the clock on the dash. "Maybe I should do this part."

"Nope, I've got it." Ventura sent the car's rear tire into the curve with a lurch, then rammed the pedal. She sharply yanked the wheel to the left and they bolted forward. A taxi blew its horn, its driver yelling an insult in some foreign tongue.

Jason drew a breath, his eyes wide. "Well, don't stop in the middle of the street. Keep going!"

And she did, taking off with a squeal as Jason clung to his shoulder harness.

Later that afternoon, Ventura drove the kids to their lessons. She checked her rearview mirror, spying them nestled in matching car seats. Little Ricky held his violin case, while Elisa clutched a soccer ball. Ventura's eyes flitted to the GPS, thinking things weren't going too badly. They were nearly to their first destination and hadn't had a mishap yet. Not only that, the kids appeared to be finally warming up to her.

"We want Jason!" Ricky whined suddenly out of nowhere. She checked her mirror to see his little lips pushed out in a pout.

"Jason's writing a business proposal," she said evenly. "I already told you."

"What about us?" Ricky asked combatively.

Ventura spoke in an effort to reassure him as well as herself. "Your dad thinks I can handle that," she said, bringing their vehicle to a halt at a traffic light.

Seconds later, Ricky yelped. "Stop!"

Ventura glanced in the backseat to see Elisa grabbing Ricky's violin case.

"Elisa, be nice."

She defiantly met Ventura's eyes, then bopped Ricky over the head with her soccer ball.

The boy hollered, "Ow!"

"Elisa!"

A horn blared behind her, and Ventura saw the light had turned green. She drove forward just as the SUV's wireless phone began ringing. She pressed a button to answer it, thinking it might be Richard or Jason.

"He pinched me!" Elisa yelled.

"Ricky!" Ventura said.

"Ventura?" It was Charles on the other end of the line. "Is this a bad time?"

"She's a meanie!" Ricky hollered from the back. "Meanie-Meanie Jelly-Beanie!"

Just then, several more horns blared, and Ventura rammed her foot on the brake. The SUV skidded forward and dragged to a stop, inches shy of hitting another car's bumper. "The worst," Ventura told Charles, breathless with fright. "I'll have to call you back."

Two and a half hours later, Ventura limped from the SUV, feeling like she'd just emerged from Boot Camp.

Jason paused on the steps to Richard's townhouse, clutching an express mail package. "Everything all right?" he asked, studying Ventura unsurely.

"Oh yeah, fine! Just fine," she said, tugging each of the children by the hand and leading them indoors.

His eyes flitted to the curb to survey the SUV for damage, before his face became awash with relief. "I'll be back in thirty minutes," he told her, scampering away.

Ventura herded the kids upstairs and toward their rooms.

"Now remember to change quickly!" she told them. "Your clothes are all laid out for you on your beds."

The kids disappeared, and Ventura picked up the heavy laundry basket on the floor with a sigh. Did the wash never end around here? She'd put everything away except for Richard's clothes. She'd do that now while Elisa and Ricky were getting ready and before Richard came home. Ventura strode to the master suite, thinking things were coming along. She'd figured out her new cell and had already memorized the children's schedules. This made it easier for her to plan out her day, when she had a good grasp on the order of her duties.

Ventura was halfway through the door when she stopped short. There, straight in front of her, standing half-nude before his dresser was…Richard!

His chest was muscled and broad, taut abs constricting. "Ventura," he said, turning toward her with a jerk. "What are you doing here?" He wore crisp white shorts, tennis socks, and shoes. A tennis racket case lay on his bed. His very big bed. The one he probably slept in half-naked—at least.

Ventura swallowed hard, her face on fire. Her palms pooled with sweat, loosening her grip on the basket handles.

"I was just putting away the laundry," she offered lamely.

He glanced at the basket in her hands. "I see."

Ventura felt something weighty smack her left foot and looked down to see she'd dropped the basket. It spilled over, balled-up pairs of socks escaping in all directions. "I'll get that," she said, mortified.

But as she raced forward, so did he. "It's all right. Let me."

Before she knew it, Ventura's toe caught on—*oh please, not that*—a pair of Richard's plaid boxers, and she stumbled forward.

"Ventura!" he called, reaching out to catch her.

"Richard!" she screeched, crashing into him.

He grabbed her around the waist and shored her up, steadying her frame against his gloriously rock-hard chest.

"Are you okay?" he asked, looking down at her with deep dark eyes.

She nodded and collected herself. "Yeah," she said, barely breathing the word.

"Good." He straightened her, then let her go.

"I'm so sorry," she babbled apologetically. "I had no clue you were in here."

"I had no idea you and the kids were back. It's my fault, really. I should have shut the door."

"No harm done," she said, backing away, her cheeks still flaming hot.

"None at all," he agreed as he watched her with a curious expression.

As she turned to leave, he stopped her. "Ventura?"

She stared at him, her heart pounding.

"Do you think I could have my shorts back?"

Ventura gasped and looked down in horror, spying Richard's underwear twisted snugly around her shoe.

Chapter Seven

"That's not what most women mean when they talk about getting into their boss's shorts."

"Shut up," Ventura said with a laugh. She and Mary stood thumbing through a rack of sexy bras at a downtown lingerie shop.

"How about this one?" Mary asked, her face aglow. "This will make Charles sit up and take notice."

Ventura scrunched up her lips at the black-and-red lace bra with "peekaboo" cut-away nipples. "I'm going on a date, not a *ho down*."

"Very funny." Mary picked through the rack, producing another selection. It was cobalt blue with a hefty underwire and big push-up pads. "Well?"

"It looks…small."

Mary cocked an eyebrow. "Don't you want to put your best assets out there?"

Ventura studied her doubtfully. "I don't know."

"Come on," Mary urged. "Try it on. It will make you feel sexy."

Of all the things Ventura had been in her lifetime, *sexy* had not been among them. "It's not like Charles will be seeing it."

"Who says he has to? It's all about how you feel on the inside. That undercurrent of…*yeow*."

"Fine," Ventura said, resigned. "I'll try it on."

"Ooh!" Mary said, grabbing a few more items off the rack. "Take these too!"

A few moments later, Mary called over the dressing room wall, "So? How's it look?"

"Too tight," Ventura said, popping open the door.

Mary pushed it the rest of the way open. "Are you kidding me? You look like a brick house!"

"And that, I suppose, would be good?"

"Better than good." Mary shot her an encouraging grin. "I say, go with it."

As they stood in line for the cash register, Mary spoke as nonchalantly as she could. "So, what's the deal with the driving instructor?"

"You mean Jason?"

"Richard's personal assistant, yeah."

"That one's super organized, let me tell you. Richard calls him *the master scheduler*."

Mary casually studied her nails. "Do you think you could get him to pencil me in?"

Ventura turned toward her with a grin. "I can't believe my ears. Are you actually asking *me* to set *you* up?"

Mary met her eyes sincerely. "Something strange is happening to me. I'm worried I'm losing my touch. Guys used to be all over me. And now… Well, I don't know. Do you think it has something to do with my horoscope?"

"What about Ed? The one who works at the White House? He took you on that private tour, remember?"

Mary huffed. "Yeah, me and whole team of cheerleaders from Nevada."

"Oh!"

"And Reginald?" Ventura asked.

"The Republican intern?" Mary lowered her voice confidentially. "Got his boxers in a bunch because I said the Dems do better fashion. I mean, really," she said rolling her eyes. "Think Jackie Kennedy."

"What about George? The one from the deli?"

"Said he got tired of waiting and started dating some cappuccino girl."

"You make coffee."

Mary pointedly raised an eyebrow.

"All right. I'll ask about Jason. And you know, you might just have a chance."

Mary's face brightened. "What? Did he say something?"

"Yeah. He wanted to know where you get your mud masks."

Mary slapped her arm. "Ha-ha."

The next morning on the Metro, Ventura questioned Mary's hot idea. The bra pinched so much, she ached each time she moved. Plus it made her much too large for this complementary cobalt blue silk blouse. Richard had asked her to take the train today because he had an early teleconference and Jason was busy helping him get ready. Ventura didn't mind the Metro-to-bus connection. She was happy to do it if it helped Richard out and almost felt spoiled having had a personal chauffer her first few weeks at the new job.

She shifted in her seat, checking her smart phone. It was cool to have a gadget that allowed her to surf the Internet and scan the latest job postings. Not that Richard wasn't a dream to work for. He was the absolute best boss and far too easy on the eyes. This only complicated matters, since Ventura felt awkward about becoming attracted to her supervisor. But maybe that was normal, a crush-on-the-teacher sort of thing that could happen to any girl. The good thing was she had Charles to focus on. Charles was an eligible guy and someone who was clearly attracted to her, which was a fun new turn of events. Ventura hadn't felt longed for since… Well, she guessed, she'd never experienced that feeling at all. And it was great. Really super. Everything it was made out to be in all those romantic songs.

While Ventura was settling into her job as a nanny, it wasn't something she aspired to be forever. She had bigger plans in mind, plans concerning her writing and making her literary mark in the world. In the meantime, Richard's kids seemed to be getting easier to manage. Now that she knew Elisa collected baseball cards and Ricky loved chocolate peanut butter ice cream, she had a handle on how to get their cooperation. Ventura looked up from her phone, noticing other people on the subway car were staring at her. She couldn't for the life of her fathom why, until she felt the brisk burst of air at her chest. Ventura looked down with a start to see her too tight blouse had burst open, exposing her sexy push-up bra. She quickly tugged it shut, furiously searching her seat and the floor for the missing buttons. But her stop was upon her, and subway doors slid open. Ventura gritted her teeth and raced from the car, clutching her blouse. "Have a good day!" she told the others as they gaped.

"Jason," Ventura whispered as she made her way into Richard's kitchen, "do you have a few safety pins I could borrow?" He glanced at her hands gripping her blouse and tugging it shut.

"Um, sure. Hang on one second."

"I'll be in the bathroom," she said, heading that direction.

En route, she nearly bumped into Richard in the narrow hall.

"Everything okay?"

"Uh-huh," she said with a death grip on her blouse.

Richard angled his chin and eyed her curiously. "If it's too cold in here, I can turn up the air-conditioning."

"Oh no!" She felt herself blush fiercely as she hurried past him. "That won't be necessary."

For the first time all week, the kids had some downtime, which was good since it was Friday afternoon. All Ventura had to do was get through these next few hours; then she'd be seeing Charles for their big date.

The kids had asked her to read them some stories, which sounded ideal to Ventura at the moment. She was exhausted from a morning of birthday parties and roller skating, and that was *after* she'd picked the kids up from their ritzy year-round kindergarten program. They sat on the sofa in the den, with Ricky snuggled up on her left and Elisa on her right. After her day of running around and indulging the kids by joining them on wheels, her cushioned seat felt like heaven. Each child had picked out some books, including newer titles and a few old classics. *This won't be so bad*, Ventura thought with a yawn. She actually liked bedtime stories. Before long, little Ricky had dozed off and soon little Elisa had also slumped against her. Was it any wonder the kids were exhausted from the rapid-fire pace of the life they led? Ventura found it slightly overwhelming too. Her eyelids began to droop as the book slipped in her hands. She felt the weight of it settle in her lap as a soothing darkness closed in.

"Who's been sleeping in *my* bed?" a sexy baritone rumbled.

Someone yanked back the covers and Ventura's eyed popped open.

"Richard?" she asked, sitting up.

He sat down beside her on his king-size bed and cupped her cheeks in his hands. Her skin tingled, and her body felt warm all over. "Why, Ventura," he said in a husky whisper, "what big eyes you have."

Ventura caught her breath as his handsome face grew near.

"And your lips." He moaned like a beast of the wild. "They're to kill for."

"Die for?" she asked uncertainly.

"Yeah." His gaze delved into hers like he longed to devour her completely. "You don't know how long I've waited for this. To take you, to have all of you."

She stared up at him, her heart on fire and cheeks ablaze. "Me too, Richard. Oh, me too."

Her silk blouse gaped open, but she didn't care. In fact, she hoped he'd rip it off her completely.

"Ventura," he growled, his mouth hovering over hers. "My sweet Ventura. How I want to make you mine."

"Oh, Richard," she sighed as his mouth closed in. His lips brushed hers.

"Ventura…"

"Richard…"

"Ventura?" he said more loudly. "Can you hear me?"

Ventura opened her eyes with a start to find Richard leaning over her where she'd apparently been dozing on the sofa with both kids.

"Richard!" she yelped.

He eyed the books on the floor with a laugh. "Well, I'm not the Big Bad Wolf."

"Of course you're not," she said, straightening her blouse as the kids groggily awakened.

"Looks like you've all had quite a day."

"Ventura took us skating," Elisa said with a happy smile.

Little Ricky's eyes were wide. "She can even do it backwards!"

"Is that so?" Richard asked with a chuckle. He eyed Ventura with appreciation, and her face warmed under his perusal. "Well, how about that."

Richard watched Ventura flit around the kitchen, thinking she was mighty perky. Perhaps the nap had done her good, or maybe it was that second cup of afternoon coffee that added extra spring to her step.

"I think everything's in order," she told him, putting away the last of the clean dishes.

The kids sat at the table, companionably coloring in matching shapes on a handout, big glasses of milk and fresh-baked cookies settled before them. Although she must have baked them hours ago, the kitchen still smelled invitingly of chocolate chips. Ventura had fed the kids early and given them dessert as they finished up the last of their homework. Richard had another boring gala to attend this evening, or else he would have eaten with them. Generally he fed the kids later, after Ventura had gone. Tonight she'd done him a special favor by doing this early to spare the teenage babysitter the extra effort. A horn blew outside, and Richard glanced through the front window, seeing a car parked outside. "Guess that's my ride!" Ventura said brightly, scooping up her purse.

"Your ride?" Richard asked, perplexed. Jason usually drove Ventura home. Richard wasn't sure what was different about tonight.

Her expression was sunny, her cheeks a dusty rose. "I've got a date," she said with a happy lilt to her voice.

Richard blinked, feeling like someone had thrust an arrow through his chest. But that was absurd, wasn't it? Why would it matter to him that Ventura was seeing someone? She was pretty, smart, and funny. It only made sense, didn't it?

"A date. I see," he stated, trying to sound casual about it. "Well, I hope you have fun."

She patted each of the kids on the head, then shot him a grin. "Thanks! I'll try."

Richard cleared his throat and strode to his office to get a better look out the window. Ventura practically ran down the steps and a good-looking guy stepped from the car. Richard thought he recognized him as Ventura's date from the Tidal Basin. He was blond and built, and most assuredly single. Free as a bird to take Ventura on any sort of outing her heart desired. Ventura glanced back toward the house, and Richard stepped away from the window. Spying on the nanny! What was wrong with him, anyway? It wasn't like he couldn't have any woman in Washington. The females here were after him all the time.

He snuck back toward the window to peer out once again as Ventura and her date drove away. *Any woman in Washington but that one*, he thought with a frown. She was not only his employee, which would make seeing her improper, but she was clearly into somebody else. Richard checked the clock on his desk and saw it was time to dress in his tuxedo and put on another show. Although tonight that performance would ring extra hollow. Having a beautiful woman on his arm didn't mean nearly as much as being with someone he felt he could talk to. Someone with a sharp wit and a good brain, and he couldn't help but notice, since he was only human, a naturally pretty face and enticingly hot body. Richard drew a breath, ashamed of himself for having such thoughts about a woman he'd hired. He wondered briefly what might have happened if she'd landed a job in her field from the start and they'd met again on personal terms rather than for business. But that was silly to think of now, given how life had evolved. The best thing Richard could do was to put any notions of becoming involved with Ventura out of his mind and focus on their working together, as politely and professionally as possible.

Ventura and Charles sat in a swanky pizza place in Georgetown, swapping stories over mugs of beer. Charles glanced at her blouse, which was held together with a series of safety pins, then met her eyes.

"You look great," he told her. "Blue's your color."

"Thanks."

"So tell me. How do you like working for the Blakes?"

Ventura took a sip of her beer, then set it down. "I'd rather not talk shop tonight," she said, still mentally kicking herself for that wild fantasy/dream about Richard and her in some storybook realm. *What was that all about?*

"We can talk about anything you want. How about the Fourth of July?"

She looked at him expectantly.

"If you've never seen Washington on the Fourth, then it's a must. People take picnics down to the Capitol lawn. The National Symphony plays. There are fireworks…"

Ventura felt a grin tugging at her lips.

"Did I say something funny?"

"No, it's just that you're being so sweet. Asking me on another picnic."

"No fears. I won't let you fall in the Reflecting Pool."

Ventura laughed happily.

"I'll pack our supper…" Charles tempted, his deep blue eyes sparkling. Ventura would be a fool to say no, and she knew it. Why then did she feel halfhearted in her response?

"Sounds great. Thanks."

Later that night, Ventura and Charles stood saying good night outside her front door.

"Thanks so much for everything," she told him. "I had a really good time."

"So did I." He studied her with a smile. "You're very easy to talk to, you know."

"You too."

He stepped toward her, and Ventura subconsciously inched back.

Then he withdrew, and she moved forward.

They continued this chicken dance a moment before both burst out laughing. He extended his hand, and she shook it.

"Well, good night," she said, "and thanks again."

"I'll call you about the Fourth," he said.

Richard returned from his gala completely worn out. He relieved the babysitter, then picked up the few odds and ends that were still scattered around downstairs. Noting a couple of children's books lying on the living room floor, he scooped them up, recognizing them as the stories the kids had been reading with Ventura. He loosened his tie and carried the books upstairs. He'd set them on his nightstand, then shelve them properly in the kids' rooms in the morning once Ricky and Elisa were awake.

He sat heavily on his bed and kicked off his shoes, thinking he was growing tired of these society things. While it was important for him to attend and stay connected, he wagered he'd have a lot more fun going with someone he could actually talk to. Somebody warm and witty, who looked like a house on fire in a blue blouse pinned together with safety pins. Feeling too tired to even slip out of his clothes, Richard settled back on the bed for a moment, propping himself up with some pillows. *I'll just flip through some of these stories for a sec,* he told himself. *Then, I'll get the motivation to get ready for bed.*

Two hours later, Richard awakened with a jolt, greeted by the blazing lights in his bedroom. A storybook lay splayed against his chest, and he still wore his tuxedo shirt and slacks. *I must have dozed off,* he thought, slapping the storybook shut. In a flash, he remembered his torrid dream. He set the book aside in shock, feeling his temperature spike. *Papa Bear?*

Chapter Eight

Richard and Ventura stood in his kitchen, stuffing sandwiches into backpacks.

"I really appreciate you working Saturday," he said. "It's beyond the call."

"Well, you certainly couldn't handle both kids on a bike all on your own. Besides, I'm happy to support anything that gets the kids outdoors—where a team sign-up isn't involved."

He smirked at her but didn't mind the ribbing. In truth, Ventura had been a breath of fresh air for all of them. She'd convinced Richard not to renew a few of their activities so Ricky and Elisa would have more time for what she called *kid stuff,* like playing hide-and-seek and setting up forts using lots of linens. Richard wasn't bothered by the mess. It made the house seem more inviting somehow. Like an honest-to-goodness family lived there.

All week long he'd been trying to come up with an excuse to see Ventura during the weekend. He'd become used to her being around during the week, and—the truth was—when she wasn't here, nothing seemed right. The kids got restless and grumpy, and Richard could never think up enough activities to entertain them. It was particularly hard when they protested they didn't like doing things without Ventura. While he'd never tell his kids, Richard secretly felt that way too.

"Jason sometimes comes with us," Richard said. "But this weekend he has plans."

"I *know*," Ventura said with a sly smile. She was thrilled that when she'd mentioned Mary to Jason, he'd taken an immediate interest. He'd asked for her number right off the bat, and now the two of them were off eating crabs in Maryland.

"He works hard," Richard said. "He deserves a life."

She looked at him thoughtfully. "I suppose we all do."

Richard appeared suddenly unnerved by her stare.

"I can babysit at night sometime," she offered. "I mean, if you'd like to get out."

"That's really nice, Ventura. I'm just not sure where I'd go or who I'd go with."

"Richard?" she said, pointing to his backpack. "I think you just put a box of butter in there."

His temples reddened. "Oh, right. Pretty silly of me," he said, taking it back out and popping it in the fridge.

Meanwhile, Mary and Jason sat at a long wooden table in the small village of St. Michael's, Maryland. They were outside on a dock abutting the water, surrounded by groups of others chatting happily and drinking beer. Newspaper had been spread out on the table before them. Heaps of freshly steamed crabbed sat in mounds ready for the taking. Jason handed Mary a small hammer and a pick. She stared at him in horror.

"They still look alive."

"Oh, they're dead, all right," he said, selecting a large one and snapping off the legs. He sucked out some of the white meat extending from a joint. "And tasty."

Mary's felt the blood drain from her face as she primly arranged her legs under the table. She wore strappy high-heeled sandals, a pretty yellow sundress, and a big floppy hat to match. "When you said you were taking me out for crabs, I thought you meant at a restaurant. You know, with margaritas?"

Jason laughed lightly and popped his crab in two at its breastplate. A fine liquid spurted forth and Mary jumped back.

"Sorry," he said with an apologetic grin. He studied the table in front of her, then met her eyes. "You haven't touched yours."

"I…um." Mary stared down at the tiny creature that appeared to stare back.

"Blue crabs are the best." To prove it, Jason pried a nice hunk of meat from his shell and held it up to Mary's mouth. She leaned forward to take a bite, and my, wasn't it delicious. So fresh and tasty. If only she hadn't seen where it had come from. It was practically cannibalistic, tearing these tiny bay creatures apart.

Jason lifted an eyebrow. "Never done this before, have you?"

Mary took a swig from her bottle of beer, steeling her nerves. "Of course I have," she said with a little laugh. "It's just been a while."

"Hmm." Jason smiled. "Tell you what, why don't I do the first one for you."

All of them would be good, Mary thought but didn't say. Besides the fact that the process turned her stomach, she'd just gotten her nails done yesterday. She adjusted the brim of her hat, devising a plan. "I kind of liked it when you fed me that bite," she said saucily.

"Did you now?" he replied, clearly intrigued. He took a sip of his own beer and set it down. "Want to try that again?"

Mary nodded, and Jason prepared her another perfect morsel. "Yummy!" she said in an effort to encourage him.

Jason reached for another crab, then met her gaze. "You're planning to have me do this all night, aren't you?"

Mary wrinkled her brow and asked weakly, "Do you mind?"

"Nope." He leaned forward to give Mary a quick peck on the lips, and her whole world brightened. "Not one bit."

Ventura and Richard glided down the path with Elisa seated on the back of Ventura's bike and Ricky situated behind his father. As they approached the water, Ventura spied a whole host of rides up ahead of them. There was a merry-go-round, a mini roller coaster, and even a Ferris wheel, its bright lights twinkling in the twilight. Cheery music played as groups of families ushered children into lines, many of them holding big puffs of cotton candy.

Ventura paused her bike, and Richard dismounted beside her.

"What's going on?" she asked, admiring the pretty display reflecting in the Potomac before them.

He got Ricky off his bike, then steadied Ventura's so she could likewise dismount and help Elisa down.

"It's the summer carnival." He stared at the scene a bit wistfully. "Vicky and I used to come down here sometimes. I'd forgotten all about it until just now." He'd planned a simple outing for the four of them, an evening picnic in the small park bordering the river. But maybe this was even better.

"Can we go?" Ricky asked, his gaze hopeful.

Richard glanced uncertainly at Ventura. "I don't think Ventura had planned to stay that long."

"But I want to get my face painted." Elisa tugged at Ventura's hand with a pleading look. "Puleeze, Ventura?"

"Pretty please?" Ricky begged.

Ventura's face brightened as she looked from one of them to the other. "I'd love to," she said with smile.

Ventura, Richard, and the kids wound through the crowd past a stage where musicians played. The children had painted faces and held helium balloons.

"I think I've had about all the fun I can handle," Richard said to Ventura. "How about you?"

"But we haven't done the Ferris wheel!" Ricky protested.

"Yeah!" Elisa said.

Richard glanced at Ventura, and she shrugged in agreement. "No fair's complete without the Ferris wheel."

Richard held up a hand. "All right. I can see when I'm outnumbered."

A few moments later, he held back the door to the small compartment. "Okay, kids, hop in!" They scrambled aboard. "Ventura?" he prodded, politely waiting for her to board next.

"Oh no, I wasn't planning to ride," she said. "I'll just watch from below."

Ricky and Elisa begged together, "But you've got to come. *Pu-leeze?*"

Richard wryly twisted his lips. "Now who's outnumbered?"

"Okay," she said with a laugh, "you've got me. But I'm going to warn you, I'm a little scared of heights."

"No worries," Richard said, meeting her eyes. "You'll have me right beside you."

Both kids sat together, which meant Richard would have to join Ventura on her side.

Ventura grinned tightly and tried not to think of that movie where the entire Ferris wheel broke loose and rolled into the ocean. Of course, this was just the Potomac River here.

She uncertainly climbed inside, and Richard joined her, pulling the compartment door shut until it latched.

Suddenly, the Ferris wheel lurched, sending their car swinging sideways.

"Whee!" Ricky and Elisa cried as they began to rise into the air.

Ventura clutched her seat with both hands, fearing she might faint.

"It's all right, I've got you," Richard said, bringing his arm around her. He gave her shoulder a light tug and motioned with his chin. "Look over there."

Now that the sun had set, the view of the carnival reflected in the water was even more magical.

"I see a boat!" Elisa cried.

"Two!" Ricky echoed.

"Those are dinner-cruise ships," Richard explained.

The scenery took her breath away. "It's beautiful."

Richard turned his face toward hers, capturing her in his gaze. "Yes."

A light breeze rippled over them, and Ventura's heart stilled. If it had been only the two of them, she wasn't sure what might have happened next. By the look in Richard's eyes, it would have been a kiss.

The car made its way back down, music and lights swirling around them. Then they were sky-bound again, rising and falling over and over together. Richard snuggled her in and held her close and Ventura's heart beat faster as Richard's warmth beside her provided comfort and stability in the night. Suddenly, the Ferris wheel jerked to a halt, startling Ventura. "What are they doing?"

Richard held her tighter. "Letting people off."

The kids' faces fell. "Aw," they said together, obviously not ready for the ride to end. And they weren't the only ones. Ventura could have stayed here all night.

There was a loud squeak; then their compartment started to lower.

"Going down," Richard announced.

I most certainly am, Ventura thought, stunned by the revelation. *Going down and falling fast.*

The moment they got home, Richard and Ventura readied the kids for bed. They were exhausted from all the fun, and both dropped off to sleep immediately.

"Ventura," Richard said as they quietly crept down the stairs. "About the Ferris wheel…"

She halted on a lower step and gripped the railing. "You don't have to say anything."

"I know, but I shouldn't have. I got carried away, I guess. The day…the bike ride…the river."

Ventura met his eyes. "Richard, you didn't do anything wrong."

"No, but I wanted to."

"Richard…"

"Ventura," he said sincerely. "I think you're terrific. Wonderful in about a million ways. But the thing is, you're employed here."

"I know."

"Which means…" He ran a hand through his hair. "I'm making a total mess of this, aren't I?"

"No."

He turned toward her, nearly pinning her to the railing, and Ventura's pulse raced. Oh, how she wanted him to take her in his arms and kiss her, the way he'd seemed to want to on the Ferris wheel. The way he appeared to need to now.

"I understand you're involved with someone," he said, his voice gravelly.

"Charles," she said weakly.

"That's just another reason this is wrong." He pursed his lips and turned away. When he looked back at her, there was a sad resignation in his eyes. "I don't want to lose you as a nanny. Elisa and Ricky would be devastated."

"I don't see how anything's changed," she said, when in truth she knew that everything had.

"Can I call you a cab?"

"That would be a good idea."

"Ventura? What are you doing?" Mary asked, striding into the room and dropping her big floppy hat onto the bed. Ventura sat on the sofa with a whole box of fortune cookies on the coffee table before her. She'd cracked open nearly every one.

She kept pulling crescents apart and examining their slips of paper. "Looking for something."

"But I thought you said the ones from the grocery store were no good? The special ones came from

Chinese take-out?" Ventura nodded toward the kitchen, and Mary peeked around the corner, spying two huge grocery bags from Zen's stuffed to the brim. Mounds of broken fortune cookies littered the kitchen table, stacks of fortunes piled high.

Mary drew a breath and came and sat beside Ventura on the sofa. "Okay. What's going on?"

Ventura looked her way. "Did you know that nine out of ten of these are repeats?"

"Well, no. Not specifically. But I guess now that you say so, it makes sense. It's like a Magic Eight Ball, right? There are probably a set number of responses. Predictions. Whatever."

Ventura set her jaw. "But in fourteen years there's a single fortune I've only gotten once." And this hadn't been for lack of trying. Ventura had probably opened more fortunes cookies than any other girl on planet Earth. She'd convinced herself long ago that if she could only find that same fortune again, she'd be able to take her first receiving it as less of a sign. But the truth was her receiving it at age eleven had been a defining moment. The fortune promised her a certain kind of future, while her father had proved in person that fairy-tale futures don't exist.

After he'd left for Kenya, Ventura had never seen him again. Not even once. At first, he'd sent post cards. One from Mozambique, another from Nepal... He was traveling around the world, making his way as a journalist and forgetting all about his family. Ventura's sister later learned their dad had made a new one. He'd married someone from Scotland and now lived Brazil, with a much younger set of kids that he shared with his brand new wife. Ventura, Hope, and her mom were collateral damage in his journalistic ambition. She'd never really understood how he could have been heartless enough to leave them, when that wasn't the father she remembered. Over the years, Ventura grew to sadly understand that the man she'd recalled was just an illusion. She'd never really known her dad at all.

Mary glanced back toward the kitchen where hordes of fortunes plastered the refrigerator. "Which one is it?"

"It's not in there."

"No?"

"I keep the special one in my wallet. With me all the time."

"What does it say?"

Ventura shook her head. "I'd rather not talk about it."

"Why not?" she said, her voice tinged with hurt. "I'm your best friend."

Ventura studied her kindly. "Of course you are. And I wouldn't change that for the world."

"Then why…?"

"It's personal, you know? So personal that it's almost become a secret wish."

"You mean, like the kind someone makes on their birthday when blowing out candles?"

"Like that exactly."

"You're afraid if you tell me, it won't come true."

Ventura felt her chin tremble. "Oh, Mary, what if it never comes true?" She hunched forward with a sob, and Mary wound her arms around her.

"Hey, you listen to me. If it's a good one, then it's bound to. You're a great person, Ventura. You deserve good things. They'll happen. Just you wait and see."

"I think I love Richard!" Ventura wailed.

Mary pulled back with a start and met Ventura's bleary eyes. "What? You mean, you're still crushing on him?"

"No!" Ventura sniffed. "I mean, I want to have his babies."

Mary's eyes went wide. "Ricky and Elisa?"

Ventura nodded, tears streaming from her eyes. "And other ones too."

"Oh my God." Mary tugged Ventura back toward her chest and hugged her tight. "How on earth did this happen? What about Charles?"

"I don't know," Ventura said with a whimper. "He's such a great guy!"

Mary patted her back. "Does Richard feel the same?"

There was silence as Ventura collected her thoughts.

"Ventura?" Mary asked again. "Does Richard feel the same?"

She broke Mary's embrace and grabbed a napkin off the coffee table to dab her eyes. "He wants me to stay the nanny."

"Ha!" Mary said, indignant. "So what? He can have his cake and eat it too?"

"No, nothing like that. He wants us to continue as we were. Totally on the level."

"Can you do that?" Mary asked with concern.

Ventura drew a breath. "I don't know."

Mary stared out the window for a prolonged beat, as if considering something. "Ventura," she finally said, "there's something I've been meaning to tell you, but I wasn't sure how you'd take it."

"Go on."

"There's a new opening at the *Daily Globe*."

"Really?"

"I've hesitated in mentioning it because you've been so happy at Richard's."

For the first time in the past few hours, Ventura felt hopeful. "But it's in journalism, right?"

"In a way." Mary grimaced. "Actually, I'm hiring my replacement."

Ventura blinked. "Mary," she said with quick understanding. "You've been promoted?"

"To Editorial Assistant," Mary said, smiling proudly.

"That's terrific."

"Thanks. So you'll consider it?"

Ventura stared at her as the weight of Mary's words sank in. Ventura might finally have an opportunity to break into journalism. While working as an administrative assistant certainly wasn't ideal, it would be a start. Still, she felt conflicted about leaving Ricky and Elisa. She'd truly grown attached to those kids…and, obviously, far too attached to their father.

"How soon do you need to know?"

Chapter Nine

Nanette stood in the foyer, dressed in a white-and-blue top and bright red hot pants that showcased her varicose veins. "Are you girls sure you won't change your minds?" she asked as they scurried toward the door with a picnic basket. "Kevin has some really nice friends."

"I'm sure," Mary whispered to Ventura with a giggle.

Ventura smiled brightly. "We already have dates, Nanette. Remember?"

"Oh, that's right," she said with a pleased purr. "One of them's on account of me."

Yes. Ventura amazingly owed it to Nanette that she'd met Charles. And Mary had Ventura to thank for meeting Jason. Now the four of them would be double dating for the Fourth. Mary had packed supper for her and Jason, while Charles had promised Ventura a special picnic. She was looking forward to this day and getting far away from thoughts of working for the Blakes. She was still considering Mary's generous offer and was nearly certain she would take it. Of course, she'd need to apply and likely compete against others. It wasn't a done deal, but having Mary influence the hiring would certainly help.

"We'll see you later," Mary told Nanette, hurrying out the door. It was a short walk to the Capitol, where they'd be meeting the boys. Ventura could hear the National Symphony tuning up already. The weather was pleasantly warm, with a light breeze blowing as dusk closed in. Ventura hadn't seen Richard since their night on the Ferris wheel. It had been nearly a week now, but somehow, between downtown meetings and stints at the office, he'd managed to keep himself hidden. Well, maybe that was for the best. She needed time to forget about being in his arms, and space to explore her budding relationship with Charles. He'd texted her all week in anticipation of this event, wanting to ensure that his plans for homemade pesto, wine, and cheese suited her taste. Ventura felt lucky to have met someone as nice as Charles and was sure that—given the chance to know him better—she would like him even more.

They circled the Capitol building, heading for its West Lawn. "Ready for our big date?" Mary asked with a grin.

"Yes, ma'am," Ventura said, nudging Mary's basket.

The sun sank low as purple and orange ribbons of color streaked the horizon. Beyond the Reflecting Pool and the long expanse of lawn dividing the various museums, the Washington Monument rose proudly in the sky, its single red eye blinking like a beacon. A crowd of Capitol Hill staffers in khaki shorts strode by, mixing in with family groups representing different nationalities and kids waving miniature American flags. A light wind picked up as twilight fell. Ventura pulled a sweater from her bag and slipped it on.

"How's your wine doing?" Charles asked, motioning to her paper cup. "Care for some more?"

"Just a bit," she said with a smile. A group of Indian women in saris strolled by, the colorful fabric fluttering in the breeze. As the last swath of cloth sailed by, Ventura caught her breath. It was Richard, sitting not that far away with his two darling kids and a gorgeous, dark-haired woman. The adults sat on portable lawn chairs, smiling happily as the twins played on a blanket by their feet. Richard raised his cup to take a sip, his gaze locking on Ventura's.

"Have either of you seen the fireworks here before?" Jason asked the girls.

"Only on TV," Mary answered.

"Then you're in for a treat." He followed Ventura's gaze across the lawn. "Well, what do you know? There's Richard."

Ventura bit her bottom lip. "Yes."

Charles looked at her pleasantly. "Do you want to go over and say hi?"

Ventura returned her attention to her date. "Not just yet."

The National Anthem began to play, and everyone rose to their feet. After the dramatic ending, the sky behind the Monument suddenly exploded in color, accompanied by huge booms and spiraling squeals. "It's gorgeous," Ventura said in awe.

Charles took her hand. "I was hoping you'd like it."

Jason stood with his arm around Mary, holding her close. "Anybody up for champagne?" Mary asked.

Ventura stole a glance in Richard's direction but couldn't spy him through the crowd. "Champagne sounds great," she said.

Mary took the chilled bottle from its carrying case, dried it off with a towel, then unscrewed the wire holders that bound the cork. She struggled to work it free with all her might, but it wouldn't budge.

"Here, let me," Ventura offered, flashing the boys a grin. Who wanted to be the weak woman asking guys to open the bubbly? She was strong enough to do it herself.

She laid the towel over the cork and gave it a sharp tug. *Pop! Whoosh!* The cork rocketed out and hit Ventura smack in the forehead. "Ow!"

"Oh my gosh, Ventura," Charles said, leaning over her. "Are you all right?"

She slowly raised her hand to her forehead, then winced at the pain. A huge knot was forming already.

"Let me get you some ice," Charles offered.

"No, I'll get it," she said, handing him the bottle and standing. "The rest of you go on and get started."

Ventura walked back from the drink vendor, clutching a bag of ice to her brow as lines snaked from the refreshment stands.

"Look, Dad!" Ricky called. "It's Ventura."

Richard turned from where they stood in line, his face registering concern. "Ventura? What happened?"

"It was just a little thing with a runaway cork."

She lifted the ice pack, revealing her welt.

"Does it hurt too badly?"

"I'll be all right."

"I thought I saw you sitting over there with your boyfriend but wasn't sure."

"Charles?"

"Isn't he the one who picked you up at the house? The one who took you boating?"

"Yes."

He studied her a moment before speaking. "I guess it's good we ran into each other this way. I've been trying to catch you all week."

"You have?" she asked with surprise.

"But between meetings and your running the kids' schedules, we always seemed to miss each other."

Ventura swallowed hard, fearing some sort of bad news was coming.

"I wanted you to know I'm taking some time away." Ventura glanced at Ricky, whose face hung long.

"Away?" she asked, not understanding.

"I thought it would be good…" He met her gaze. "For the best, I mean, if I took some time to get reacquainted with Gloria."

"Gloria," Ventura said, thinking of the pretty brunette.

"Daddy always goes away with Gloria," Ricky said with a pout. "He never takes us."

Richard thumbed his nose. "Now you know that's not true. You're just not coming this time, all right?"

"How long will you be gone?" Ventura asked.

"A week. Maybe two."

"I see."

"Jason will help keep everything under control."

"When are you leaving?"

He held her gaze a prolonged beat.

"In the morning."

Ventura returned to the picnic blanket, where the other three toasted to the country's birthday with paper cups. Mary shot her a worried glance. "Are you okay?"

Ventura sat and put down the ice pack. "I'll live."

Charles warmly patted her shoulder.

"It's too bad that happened," Jason said kindly. "But it will heal up."

"I ran into Richard." Ventura met Jason's eyes. "He said he's going away tomorrow."

"You mean you didn't know until now?" Jason asked with alarm. "I thought for sure Richard had…" He twisted his lips in thought. "That's weird."

"Who'll look after the kids?" Charles asked.

"I'll stay with them at night," Jason said. "And Ventura will still be there in the daytime."

Mary shot Ventura a pointed look, and she returned it.

After a beat, Ventura tilted her champagne toward the others. "To birthdays and new beginnings."

Charles's expression warmed. "I'll drink to that."

"Another one. Come on," Ricky pleaded.

"Yeah!" Elisa gazed up at her with big brown eyes. "*Pu-leeze?*"

Nearly two weeks had gone by and Ventura had run through the kids' regular stack of storybooks days ago. So, she'd turned to inventing stories for them instead, which they seemed to like even better.

The kids were dressed in their pajamas and snuggled up beside Ventura on Elisa's bedroom window seat. "What will it be tonight?" she asked them. "The sequel to the castle saga, or something spooky… Say, *Mystery of Magic Mountain?*"

"The sequel," Elisa chirped.

"Ghosts!" Ricky demanded.

Ventura laughed, hugging them both warmly. "How about one of each, then?"

The children nodded, appearing cherubic, and Ventura's heart sank. She'd applied for the job at the *Globe* yesterday morning. With any luck, she'd get an interview and land the position, which would mean her starting there in a couple of weeks. While Ventura hated leaving the children, she understood that being a nanny wasn't her chosen career long-term. She'd studied for something specific. She needed to test those wings and see if she could soar.

"I'll bet Daddy would like these," Elisa said, snuggling under her arm.

"When's he coming home?" Ricky asked.

"Soon," Ventura said with a smile.

"We like you a whole lot better than those other nannies," Elisa informed her.

"Yeah," Ricky said, grinning sweetly. "We think Daddy does too."

Ventura felt her cheeks warm in spite of herself.

"Somebody having a pajama party in here?"

Ventura looked up to see Richard standing in the threshold. He appeared more handsome than ever with his skin burnished in a bronze cast that said he'd been spending lots of time outdoors.

The kids leapt from the window seat and raced to him. "Daddy!" they cried, hugging him soundly as he bent low to scoop them into his arms. "We missed you!"

"Well, good," he said, thumbing each of their noses, "because I missed you." He glanced in Ventura's direction. "All of you."

Ricky gave his dad an earnest gaze. "Ventura tells the best stories."

"She does, does she?" Richard asked, standing.

Ventura hung her head with a blush. "Oh no, they're not really—"

"Yes, they are!" Elisa assured her dad, giving his hand a tug. "The very best."

"About castles and monsters…"

"Princesses," Elisa chimed in.

"And *ghosts*," Ricky added, lowering his voice in an eerie tone.

Richard chuckled, then met Ventura's eyes. "Sounds like I'll have to hear one of these stories."

"We were just about to hear one now," Ricky said.

"Two," Elisa corrected.

Richard raised his brow at Ventura. "Mind if I stay?" he asked, taking a chair.

Ventura saw there was no way out of this now. "Of course not," she said, smiling tightly.

Twenty-five minutes later, Richard leaned forward, resting his elbows on his knees and just as engaged as his children.

"And with that," Ventura finished, "Andorra the warrior knight knew she held the silver key. The key to the kingdom she'd only known—up until then—in her dreams. Now, all she had to do"—she shot Ricky and Elisa a wink—"was open the door."

"Yeah!" the kids shouted with glee.

Richard clapped his hands in applause. "Wonderful, Ventura. I don't know how you did that."

She felt her cheeks warm. "It was only a story."

"No," he told her. "It was more than that. You managed to capture us all and completely carry us away."

Ventura beamed. "Thanks."

"How many do you have?" Richard asked her.

"Stories? Oh I don't know." She gave a light laugh. "I can't really put numbers on my imagination."

"Fascinating," he said. "Have you thought of writing any of them down?"

Ventura stared at him. "Like, for…?"

"Publication." He looked at Ricky and Elisa. "What do you think, kids? Don't you believe Ventura could make her own storybooks?"

"Yeah," Ricky said.

"And better than the ones over there," Elisa agreed, pointing across the room.

Richard turned his expectant gaze back on Ventura.

"I don't know," she said. "I've never really thought about it."

"Well, I know good storytelling when I hear it. I'm an editor, aren't I?" He rubbed his palms together and stood from his chair. "But for now, I see two little munchkins who've stayed up past their bedtimes." He glanced at Ventura. "You're here a bit late yourself."

"I've been staying on to help Jason," she told him. "The kids asked for me to be here at bedtime." She shrugged. "I hated to disappoint."

"No. I'm sure you wouldn't do that." He eyed her thoughtfully. "You could never disappoint any of us."

A little while later, Ventura was about to sneak out the front door when Richard stopped her. He'd apparently relieved Jason the moment he got home. And Jason, being eager to finally spend an evening with Mary, had quickly taken off.

"I want to thank you for all you did to help with the kids while I was gone," he said as they stood in the foyer.

"I was happy to do it," she answered honestly. "Elisa and Ricky are very special."

"I agree."

"I'm glad you had a good vacation."

He met her eyes with a soulful gaze. "I needed some time to think."

"I'm sure Gloria helped."

"Absolutely. Nothing clears my head like spending time on the water."

"Water?"

Richard stared at her dumbfounded. "Gloria's my boat."

"*Boat?*"

"Didn't anyone…? Why, of course, why would they have… What I mean is…" He blinked hard. "You didn't know?"

Ventura shook her head. "I thought Gloria was the woman you were with on the Fourth?"

"You mean Jenny?" Richard slapped his forehead. "I'm so sorry, Ventura. I haven't been very clear about any of this. Gloria's the sailboat I keep on the Chesapeake Bay. I've referred to her as a *she* for years. It never even occurred to me. Oh gosh. You thought that Jenny was Gloria and that she and I…?" He sputtered a laugh. "Ventura, Jenny's my *sister*."

Ventura's mouth hung open. "Sister?"

"The kids' aunt. She's in law school in New York but was visiting for the holiday."

"Oh," Ventura said, feeling the blood drain from her face. She felt suddenly weakened, as if she might faint at any moment from sheer information overload. "Then, you and she…?"

He vehemently shook his head. "I'm sorry about Gloria. I should have explained."

"You don't really need to explain your personal life to me."

He stepped toward her. "Don't I?"

"Richard, I have something to tell you." She felt she should let him know she'd applied for another job and that he might soon need to shop for a new nanny.

But could she really do that tonight? His first night home, when he looked like sin in a suntan and was close enough to kiss her once again? She involuntarily licked her lips, aching to taste his. He wasn't taken after all. Had no other woman on the horizon, just some silly old boat. She imagined him helping her aboard and sailing her away to some faraway place that was made for just the two of them. Four of them, counting the kids.

"What is it?" he asked, his voice husky.

Ventura felt herself losing her nerve.

"Maybe we should talk about it tomorrow."

"If that's what you want."

Ventura's cell buzzed, and she checked it, seeing it was Charles. He was letting her know he'd arrived to pick her up and was parked by the curb outside.

"I've got to go." She broke away from Richard's gaze, hoping she was doing the right thing. Leaving the life she'd built here and embarking on another one. But inwardly, Ventura knew she couldn't stay at the Blakes' forever. The more she was around Richard, the harder it was to resist him. Instinct told her that he was growing attracted to her too. But what did that mean in their current state, especially when she was still seeing Charles?

Ventura hurried toward Charles's car, her head swirling and her heart pounding. She'd once believed twenty-five was the age at which one knew everything. Now she saw it was a time when she knew nothing at all. Except for how to make a great big mess of everything. She had a chance for happiness with Charles, and he clearly wanted to spend time with her. She didn't need to go chasing some silly dream about the one man who'd already told her he couldn't become involved.

"Are you all right?" Charles asked as she fastened her seat belt.

Ventura glanced back toward the house, her eyes moist. "Yeah, thanks," she said, stealthily wiping back a tear. "I'm fine."

Chapter Ten

"Ventura," Richard told her the next morning in his home office. "I've been thinking about last night."

"You have?"

"About your stories."

"Oh."

"I was serious when I urged you to write them down. I have a nose for these things. I think you have potential."

"But I was trained in news writing. I wouldn't have a clue how to go about—"

"Come on, if you can speak it, you can write it. You're a good writer to boot. Professionally trained. All you'll be doing here is employing a little creative license."

"And then what?" she asked him. "I don't even know what the next step would be. Submitting to publishers? From what I hear, the hurdles are enormous."

"I have some agent friends in New York." He sincerely met her gaze. "If you'd be willing to write a few of your stories down and polish them, I might see if I can open some doors."

Her face warmed with gratitude. "That's so nice. But why would you do that for me?"

"Because I can." He shuffled through some papers on his desk, then set them aside. "Now, wasn't there something you wanted to tell me?"

She felt awful dropping the bomb on him at this moment, particularly with him being so kind about her children's stories. But she needed to go through with it.

She'd had a message on her voice mail this morning saying she was wanted for an interview. Things had started moving and might move along even more quickly from here on out.

"I feel terrible about telling you this after you've been so nice."

His face fell. "What is it? What's happened?"

She gathered her courage and pressed ahead. "I applied for a job at the *Daily Globe*."

"And?"

"I've been called in for an interview."

To her surprise, his expression brightened. "That's fantastic. What great news!"

"Huh?"

"This is what you wanted, isn't it? The whole reason you came to Washington?"

"Um, yeah. But I thought... Wait a minute. You're not upset that I'm leaving?"

He sat back with a sigh. "You're not leaving yet, are you? You said you'd just been called for an interview."

"Yeah, but I kind of have some contacts on the inside."

He laid his palms on his desk. "Even better."

Ventura flinched, feeling oddly stung by his enthusiasm. "Is it...? I mean, do you want me to go?"

He met her gaze and held it. "Honey, I've never wanted a nanny to stay so much in my life."

Ventura's cheeks flamed.

"But I've also never wanted any of them to succeed more than I do you. Ventura, this is your life. You have to go for it. I want what you want. Can't you see?"

She looked deep in his eyes and wished he knew that part of what she wanted was him. And it was too.

Her heart skipped a beat as she acknowledged the truth. She couldn't keep seeing Charles when she was desperately in love with someone else.

Jason bustled into the room, carrying some papers. "Here's the copy you asked for this morning."

"Thanks, Jason," Richard said without taking his eyes off Ventura's.

Jason looked from one of them to the other, then backed out the door.

"O-kay…" he said, pulling it shut. "I'll just close this."

"It's almost time for me to pick up the kids," Ventura said.

Richard's gaze still lingered on hers. "I don't want you to ever be afraid," he told her. "Afraid to go after your dreams. You have to stand up for your life. Everyone does."

"Do you?" she asked with a challenge. "Go for what you want?"

"I'm not sure I understand what you mean."

She pursed her lips, feeling foolish. What did she expect him to say? *I wish you'd stop seeing Charles and go out with me.* She hadn't even begun the story writing in earnest and already her thoughts were spinning off into fantasy. "I apologize," she said, standing to take her leave. "I shouldn't have said that."

The following Saturday, Ventura sat sharing a picnic with Charles at Hanes Point. Airliners glided overhead, taking off from and landing at Reagan International Airport as the waters of the Potomac stretched out ahead.

"This is awesome," Charles said, studying the view. "Another brilliant idea."

He took her hand, and Ventura's heart ached for him, because she knew what was coming. "I feel so awful about having to say this." She hung her head, and he leaned toward her.

"What's up?"

"It's us, Charles," she said, meeting his eyes. "I just can't do this."

"Did I…?" His face was etched with pain. "Was it something I said?"

She sighed heavily. "It's nothing you've done at all. Actually, you've been perfect. The most wonderful guy a girl could hope to date."

"Okay," he said, like he sensed more was coming.

"But I can't keep on seeing you when I have such strong feelings for someone else."

He looked toward the water, then slowly angled back toward her. "Richard?"

Ventura averted her gaze.

"Is it mutual?"

"It doesn't really matter," she said, turning back to him. "He's always in the way."

Charles stared at her sadly, getting it. "I see."

Mary entered the basement apartment, carting a big bag of Chinese take-out. "Ventura!" she called in a singsongy tone. "I have good news."

"That's great. I could use some right now."

Mary surveyed her sitting sadly on the sofa, like she'd lost her best friend. "What's wrong with you?"

"Charles and I broke up."

Mary set her hefty bag on the coffee table. "Uh-oh. Who ditched who?"

"I wish I could say it was mutual."

"My poor baby!" Mary cried, wrapping her arms around her.

"I dumped him."

Mary pushed back. "What?"

Ventura nodded.

"Why?"

"It's not good to see one man when all you can do is think of someone else."

"Richard." Mary shot her a sympathetic gaze. "Listen, Ventura. I know it's been hard. Unrequited love and all that. From what I hear, it's a killer. Not that I'd know personally," she added quickly. "But still, I understand that it's been painful for you, which is what makes my news extra good."

"Mary?" Ventura asked, her hopes rising.

"Yes!" Mary squealed. "You got the job!"

They hugged each other and hollered with delight until Nanette called downstairs to ask if they had men over. This was it, a happy sign that Ventura's life was turning around. She'd been right to break up with Charles. And she'd be right to move on from Richard. She needed to find her own life and forge ahead. But first, she thought, catching a whiff of crispy scallops, she was famished. "What's in the bag?"

Mary reached in the sack and dug out two fistfuls of crescents. "Extra fortune cookies," she said with a grin.

Ventura looked up at Richard as they stood in the kitchen. She'd just fixed the kids an early supper and was preparing to leave. Richard was dressed in his tuxedo, ready for another society outing. "I can't believe you understand."

"What I understand is that in this town, opportunity only knocks once. You've got to answer, Ventura. Go for it."

Ventura lowered her voice so the kids couldn't hear. "But what about Ricky and Elisa?"

"We'll manage somehow, just like we did before." He studied her a beat. "Look, if you're having doubts about taking this job, why not give it a trial run? You know, for a couple of weeks. If it turns out you're miserable there, you can come back here."

"Are you serious? You'd hold a spot open for me?"

"What are friends for?

"Oh, Richard!" she said springing into his arms. "You're the best!"

He held her to him and patted her back while Elisa and Ricky sent curious gazes in their direction. "Yeah, you too."

"Are you two getting married?" Elisa asked.

Ventura felt her cheeks blaze as she broke from Richard's embrace.

"That was just in friendship," she said, blinking at the kids.

Richard straightened his bow tie. "Absolutely."

Ricky and Elisa exchanged glances.

Ventura stared at Richard, and he stared back.

"I'm not worried if you're not," he said quickly.

Chapter Eleven

It was late at night when Ventura rapped at Nanette's bedroom door.

"It's open! Come in!"

Nanette's suitcase lay open on the bed. She was going away on some kind of romantic adventure with a man who worked for the government.

"Are you sure you'll be safe traveling with Kevin?" Ventura asked. "You really don't know that much about him."

"That's because he can't say."

"You don't think it's a little odd that he always wears those dark glasses?"

"Trust me on this," she said with a wink. "He doesn't *always* wear them."

"Well, I'm glad you're having fun," Ventura said. "Wherever you're going."

"To a resort, if you must know. If I told you which one, you'd be embarrassed."

"Oh," Ventura said with a blush. "Well, I brought you something for your trip. Something for good luck."

Nanette stared down at the package in Ventura's hand. "Oh, how sweet! You didn't have to."

"I know," Ventura said. "But you've been so good to me and Mary both. It's just a little something."

Nanette grinned and eagerly tore into the wrapping. "Chocolate fortune cookies." She giggled with delight. "Where on earth did you get these?"

"I have my sources."

"Thank you, dear." Nanette gave her a warm hug. "So, tell me, how are things going with Charles?"

"We broke up."

Nanette looked at her with surprise. "I don't understand. I thought everything was going so well."

Ventura sat on Nanette's bed with a sigh.

Nanette considered her a moment. "This is about that editor, isn't it? Richard Blake."

"Oh, Nanette, I'm not even sure if he feels the same."

"Have you thought about talking to him? Telling him the truth?"

"I couldn't! Not after all he's done for me. He's been so kind, given me so many chances. He's even gone so far as to support my writing. I don't think I told you, he sent a manuscript of mine to a couple of his agent friends in New York."

Nanette eyed her doubtfully. "You mean to say there's never been any chemistry between you?"

Ventura felt her face burn hot but held her tongue.

"I see. Well, you know what they say…" She paused a moment to toss some skimpy lingerie in her bag. "Where there's smoke, there's fire." She met Ventura's eyes. "How do you know he's not thinking the same thing? *She's such a nice young woman. She's done so much for my family. How could I possibly take advantage of her?*"

"But he wouldn't be taking advantage!" Ventura blurted out. "I'd want him to."

"Ah-ha!

Ventura hung her head. "What am I going to do?"

"Tell him when the moment is right."

"But what about my new job? And Mary? Her relationship with Jason? I wouldn't want to impact that in a bad way if things were to sour between Richard and me. Maybe I should forget all about him." She sighed heavily. "I can't imagine how this will work out."

Nanette sat on the bed beside her. "Things have a way of resolving themselves," she said kindly. "You'll see. You go on with your life. Follow your heart. Do what you're meant to do. Your destiny will catch up with you."

Ventura followed Mary with trepidation through the bustling newsroom where noise assaulted her senses. Fingers furiously tapped at keyboards, phones rang nonstop, and editors barked out orders. Ventura clutched Mary's arm as they passed by rows of disheveled reporters sitting with mugs of coffee at their computers.

Mary angled her chin toward Ventura. "Stop acting like you're in a slasher film," she hissed. "This is your dream job, remember?"

She showed Ventura to a dingy cubicle at the far recesses of the room, near the coffee-making station. "You stay here. I'll bring you something to do."

A few moments later, Mary returned and dumped some coffee packets on Ventura's desk.

"What's this?" she asked, looking up.

Mary set her hand on her hip. "Your first assignment."

Jason and the kids walked through the front gate, holding ice-cream cones. Richard looked up from his front steps, where he sat reading the newspaper.

"You know, Mary's doing a decent job with her fashion column," he said. "Not that I understand a word of it."

Jason took a bite of ice cream. "That's because you don't speak our language."

"What's that?" Richard teased. "The language of *love*?"

The kids plunked down on the front steps, licking their cones.

"How's the chocolate peanut butter?" Richard asked them.

Both kids frowned. "Nothing's the same without Ventura," Elisa said.

Ricky shook his head in agreement, and Jason glanced at Richard. "I'll bet Papa Bear knows just what you mean."

"Shut up," Richard said under his breath. He never should have told Jason about that dream he'd had. At the time, it had seemed harmless and funny. But Jason hadn't let him hear the end of it. After he'd found Ventura passed out on the sofa with those storybooks, Richard had later thumbed through them. For some reason that had led to a pretty wild dream that night. He'd been the Papa Bear, and Ventura—dressed as Goldilocks—had landed in his bed.

Jason whispered in Richard's ear, "And I thought women were the ones who had romantic fantasies."

Richard elbowed him. Hard.

"Ouch!"

"What happened, Uncle Jason?" Elisa asked.

"Just got an, uh…" He glanced at Richard. "Stitch in my side."

Jason laughed, muttering under his breath, "Man, that was pervy."

Richard snatched away his ice cream. "Hey!"

"You'd better not breathe a word of that to Mary," Richard said, knowing Mary would immediately share it with Ventura.

"I swear on my life!"

He grabbed for his cone, but Richard held it out of reach.

"Swear on your Gucci loafers."

"Aw, man, that's not fair."

Richard held the cone higher.

"Okay, okay. I swear."

"Ventura!" Mary cried with dismay. "What are you doing?"

Ventura lethargically opened one eye. "Resting."

"Well, you don't rest here, okay? Wake up!"

Ventura groggily lifted her head to see she was still in the newsroom. So it hadn't been a dream. The nightmare was real. For three weeks, she'd done nothing but mess up. The few meager copy editing assignments she'd scored had been a major botch, and she couldn't even seem to make coffee.

"Hey!" an angry voice snarled. "What idiot keeps burning the joe?"

Ventura buried her head with her arms, her cheek pressed to her metal desk. It couldn't really stay this bad forever. Could it?

Mary leaned toward her with a whisper. "You've got to find a way to snap out of it, girlfriend, or I'll be forced to hire your replacement."

Ventura slowly sat up. "But all I do is *type and file, and type and file, and...*"

"I told you, you'd have to start from the ground up."

Ventura's head dropped back on her desk with a thud as she centered her gaze on the coffeepot. "You mean grounds, don't you?"

Ventura dragged herself toward Nanette's townhouse, practically in tears. Nothing about this new job was going as planned. She'd expected it to be hard but had no idea it would prove so humiliating. She was an intelligent woman with a good education, and yet she felt like the lowest of the low in that newsroom. Perhaps it was because she *was* the lowest person on the totem pole, not to mention the newest employee.

She was just approaching the front steps when she spotted Richard's sports car parked at the curb. *Richard? What on earth is he doing here?* Suddenly invigorated, she raced up the stairs and through the front door.

She entered the townhouse to find Richard chatting in the living room with Nanette, who'd just returned from the islands.

"Richard!" Ventura said with a happy smile. "It's so great to see you." Unable to stop herself, she sprang into his arms.

He laughed warmly, hugging her back. "You too, Ventura. You look…" He gave her an appraising frown. "Tired."

"She *is* tired," Nanette assured him. "Exhausted from that horrible new job of hers."

"Nanette," Ventura warned. "It's not that bad."

"But you said—"

"What brings you to Capitol Hill?" Ventura asked, turning her attention on Richard.

"I brought you a special delivery," he said with a warm smile.

He handed her an express mail envelope, and she checked the sender, seeing it was from New York.

"Open it," Richard said.

She tore into the package and scanned through its document, unable to believe her eyes. "Is this what I think?"

He shot her a proud grin. "It's a representation agreement, from one of the best agencies in children's literature."

"Whoohoo!"

Nanette smiled broadly. "You, baby, are going to be famous."

"Well, I don't know about that." She glanced at Richard, not knowing what to say.

"If you'll give them permission to shop your work, they think they can make a deal for you. High six figures for the entire fantasy series. Ventura, do you know what this means?"

She numbly shook her head, overwhelmed by the magic of the moment.

"That you could write full-time."

Tears leaked from her eyes. "You mean, doing something I love? Like telling my stories." That seemed almost too good to be true.

"That's exactly what I mean." He reached up and stroked back her tears, and Nanette sighed loudly. "But first, you'll have to sign on the dotted line."

"I'll do it," Ventura said, her heart soaring.

Richard met her eyes. "I need you to understand, there are no guarantees. We'll have to wait awhile and see what comes through."

"I understand that." Ventura swallowed hard. "But what good is life if you can't take chances?"

For Ventura, the next few weeks didn't seem nearly as dreary. She'd finally learned to make the coffee and had been given a few more copy editing assignments, which she'd handled well. It was good to see a light at the end of the tunnel and imagine her work at the *Globe* wouldn't always involve darkness. The people were good here and helpful in moving folks along. Mary had already arranged for her to meet with an associate editor in the City Desk department, and he'd appeared impressed by Ventura's credentials. Still, it was hard to fight the lure of fantasizing about a day job that allowed her to create her own worlds and let her spirit run free.

She was sitting at her desk, working on an article revision, when her cell phone buzzed. She checked the number, seeing the call came from New York. Ventura held her breath, praying this was the call she'd dreamed of.

"Hello?" she said, picking up.

"Ventura?" It was Leon, her literary agent from Manhattan. "I hope you're sitting down."

Her heart beat faster. "I am," she said with a happy gasp.

"Because you, sweetheart, are about to make us loads of dough."

Ventura squealed, and heads swung in her direction. She spun her chair to face the coffeemaker and lowered her voice. "What's up, Leon?"

"We're talking a bidding war. A big advance. And if sales go as they're expected to, maybe even film rights down the line, audio. The whole shebang. They loved that whole spiel about the warrior princess following a quest based on fortune cookies." He blew a breath. "I hope you don't owe anyone money."

"Why's that?"

"Because they're going to come collecting on their IOUs."

Ventura blinked as the coffee dripped into its clouded carafe. "What are you saying?"

"You'll be making more moola than a twenty-five-year-old has a right to. Not that I'm complaining. I get fifteen percent."

"And you're worth every dollar," she said.

"That underwater castle thing?" he told her. "That was genius. And the role reversals with the girls taking on the traditional male roles? Yeah, that sold big. But here's what I don't get," he said in his deep Queens accent. "How it is they've got Chinese take-out under the sea?"

Ventura laughed happily. "You have to write what you know, Leon," she said, grinning broadly. "Write what you know."

Later that night, she, Mary and Nanette sat around, drinking champagne.

"I'm going to hate losing you at the paper," Mary said sadly, "but in my heart, I'm happy you're on your way."

Nanette grew misty-eyed. "And I'm going to miss having you around here."

"Nobody says I'm leaving."

"Come on, Ventura," Mary told her. "We can see the writing on the wall. You'll be making way more than you need to live in this place. You can go upscale! A place at the Watergate!"

"But I like it here," Ventura protested. There was no place she'd rather live. At least on this side of the Potomac. Her phone rang, and she saw it was Richard.

"I'm calling to congratulate you."

"Thanks so much. None of this would have happened without you."

"I don't believe that," he said. "You might have taken a different path, but you would have gone that same way eventually. I'm sure of it."

"Ricky and Elisa were a big inspiration."

"The kids miss you."

"I miss them too."

"We all miss you." There was a pause on the line; then his voice rose in a question. "Ventura? I was hoping to take you out to dinner to celebrate. I mean, you're not working for me now. And well… I hope you don't mind, but Jason told me you're no longer seeing Charles."

Ventura stared at Mary, who innocently turned away.

"That would be nice," she said.

"Can I pick you up on Saturday at seven?"

"Seven sounds fine," Ventura said with a grin.

Nanette and Mary exchanged knowing glances.

"He finally asked you out?" Mary said, sounding pleased.

Ventura nodded, still over the moon herself. She was going out *on a date* with a man she was crazy about. Head-over-heels crazy about. Now, all she had to do was think up something to wear.

"Don't worry, dear," Nanette said sweetly. "We'll help you get ready."

"Oh, no you won't!" Ventura said with a laugh. "I know you both mean well, and Mary, your fashion advice is the best. But, girlfriends, the Ventura Hart you see sitting before you today is not the one who walked in here all those weeks ago. I'm a new woman, *my own woman*. And, trust me on this," she said with a wink. "I know just what Richard likes."

Mary and Nanette stared at her, both of them beaming from ear to ear.

"Well, well," Mary said, raising her flute of champagne. "Here's to the new Ventura!" She paused a beat to study her. "Now that you mention it, it's true. You *are* dressing better." She brought a hand to her chin. "But in your style, not mine."

Nanette nodded approvingly and also lifted her glass. "I like it!"

Ventura smiled and flipped back her hair. "Why, thanks," she said, merrily clinking their glasses. "And here's to both of you, my very best friends on earth. Thanks for sticking with me in the journey."

A tear glistened in the corner of Mary's eye. "I'll always stand by you, Ventura."

"Yeah," Nanette said, swallowing hard. "Me too."

Ventura's heart brimmed with affection for the two of them. For the first time in her life, she knew what having a mother and sister felt like. She set down her glass and stretched her arms out wide. "Aw, come here," she urged the two of them. They put down their drinks as well to join her in a group hug, where they all giggled and cried and said how much they loved each other…until they finally decided to open another bottle of champagne.

Chapter Twelve

The following Saturday, Ventura and Richard strolled along the path beside the Tidal Basin. The moon rose high above, casting its reflection on the water as warm breezes blew, strumming through the cherry trees. They'd had a delicious dinner at an Argentinian restaurant: enormous grilled steaks with a wonderful bottle of wine. The conversation had flowed easily. Perhaps because they already knew each other so well. Although in some ways this was their first date, in many ways it wasn't. Ventura and Richard had been getting to know one another for quite some time. They not only shared a friendship, but a powerful mutual attraction as well. An attraction that each of them had been fighting for far too long. With the barriers that had existed between them removed, being with Richard was exhilarating. Ventura felt herself warm through and through at the thought that someone could treat her so specially. Richard made her feel just like a fairy-tale princess, and no one had made her feel that way in a while.

"Thanks for the dinner," she told him. "It was fabulous."

He stopped walking to look in her eyes. "I'm glad you're having fun. Thanks for coming out with me."

If only he knew. She'd go out with him anywhere. At any time.

"Are you chilly?" he asked as the wind picked up.

"Not a bit," she said, holding his gaze. His face was darkly handsome, haunted by shadows and the moonlight as faraway streetlamps cast a tender glow.

He turned toward her and stepped closer. "It might make me sound like a jerk, but I'm awfully glad you stopped seeing Charles."

Ventura's pulse whipped into overdrive while her cheeks burned. "I couldn't keep seeing him," she breathed. "Not when I'd developed feelings for someone else."

He smiled softly, cupping her face in his hands. "Someone?"

Ventura fell into his eyes, dark canyons that spoke of heat and fire. She nodded, and he stroked her cheek. "That's pretty amazing. I developed feelings for someone too." He pulled her closer then, taking her in his arms.

Ventura tilted up her chin as his mouth moved in. She'd wished for this moment for weeks now, but somehow had never thought it would come.

"Would you mind if I kissed you?" he asked, his voice husky.

She brushed her lips to his in acquiescence and he pulled her close, holding her firmly up against him as he devoured her mouth with his. Ventura felt lost in his kiss as her heart pounded faster. He was so warm and tender, yet passionate at once. And his passion was headily intoxicating. So intoxicating she only felt herself wanting more.

"Ventura," he said between kisses. "Come away with me."

She pushed back to gaze in his eyes. "Where?"

"I'd like you to meet Gloria."

"Your boat?" she asked with a delighted laugh.

He shot her a hopeful look. "Next Saturday? I can pick you up at four. We'll spend the whole evening on the water."

Ventura couldn't imagine anything more romantic. "Sounds perfect."

The next week, Mary and Jason scuttled down into the hold of Richard's boat. Jason passed Mary a warm bag of Chinese food as she smiled at the children. They were all wearing life vests. "Now remember," she told Ricky and Elisa. "As quiet as church mice. Not a word."

Elisa made a zipper motion across her lips, and Ricky followed.

"Good," Mary said, sending Jason a smile. "Now all we do is wait."

As they approached the slip, Ventura saw the word *Gloria* painted on the gorgeous twenty-eight-foot boat. "She's a beauty."

"She'd become a little worn from neglect," Richard confessed. "But I've spent a good deal of time here lately fixing her up."

"You were too busy to sail for a while?"

"I was too down to sail for a while," he told her honestly. "Let's say Vicky leaving kicked the wind of me." He held out his hand to help her aboard. "But it's okay. I've come back full steam now."

Ventura stepped unsteadily aboard and the boat rocked. "I don't know a thing about sailing."

"That's all right. Just follow my lead."

"Will I have to call you captain?" she teased with a grin.

"Only if you want to."

Her hair was long and loose, curly just the way he liked it. Richard had taken nearly a month planning this out, and after their date the previous weekend, he was certain he was doing the right thing. There was no one he wanted in his life more than Ventura. She was right for him. In a very special way, she was right for all of them. And not just as the nanny. The moment she'd left their house to take that job at the paper, he'd realized that.

He opened a bench seat and pulled out two life jackets. "Safety first," he said, sliding one over her head.

"Aye, aye, Captain," she said, her dark eyes sparkling.

"I like the sound of that," he said with a wink.

Ventura looked around as he readied the riggings. "Huh, that's weird."

"What?"

"For the life of me, I thought I smelled sesame chicken."

"Probably just the salt air," he said, hoisting up a sail.

Ventura wrinkled her nose. "You're probably right."

Within a half an hour, the main sail had filled and Richard had raised a colorful spinnaker before it. Ventura leaned back against a railing, enjoying the ride.

"I can see why you like it out here. It's exciting and calming at once."

"We've got the perfect day for this. Tailor-made." He glanced up at the sky and leaned into the wind. "Heads up, Ventura. She's coming around!"

"Who?" she asked as the heavy boom swung in her direction.

"Richard!" she yelped, ducking under the swing of the main sail while he cupped her head in his hand to protect it.

"You need to keep your head low when that happens."

"Now you tell me," she said, nearly breathless.

They clambered up on the other side of the boat and positioned themselves on the bench seat as Richard maneuvered the sheets. "We'll pull into that cove over there and anchor awhile," he told her, shifting the rudder ever so slightly to steer their craft in that direction.

Ventura was glad to be with someone who was knew what he was doing on the water, for she was lost completely. She'd never understood how much skill and finesse it took to captain a boat until she'd come here with Richard. She stared at him, handsomely in command of his craft, and her heart welled with emotion. She adored so many things about him. How well he did in business, the love he had for his children... The admiration he'd shown for her. Winds rippled and he met her gaze. "I hope you're having a good time."

"I'm having the best time."

"That's good." He steered the boat into a cove with a mysterious grin. "Let's hope it gets even better."

Sweat dribbled down Ventura's chest and pooled in her cleavage beneath her snug cotton shirt. They were anchored in the cove, and their main sail was down. "You should have told me to bring a swimsuit."

"I'm sorry. I didn't think of it." Richard cracked open a cooler and handed her an ice-cold beer. "I had a lot of other things on my mind."

"Gosh," Ventura said, looking around. "I can still smell it."

"Must be the algae," Richard offered helpfully. "Smells just like friend wontons."

"Really?" she asked with incredulity.

Richard fidgeted with his beer bottle, then met her eyes. "I'd like to propose a toast. To you and your literary success!"

"Why, thanks," she said, clinking his bottle. "Here's to you having a part in it."

"A very small part."

"You're just being modest."

They both drank then an awkward silence settled in, as gulls called noisily overhead. Richard took their beers and set them in holders. "I'm really happy about your book deal," he said as sunshine warmed her hair. "Really happy about everything."

"Yeah. Me too."

"I don't want you to think that I haven't thought about this, because I have—in excruciating detail."

"It was painful?" she asked, perplexed.

He stunned Ventura by reaching into a net storage compartment and extracting a small gift. "It's only going to hurt if you say no." He handed her the present and her heart pounded faster. Could she really hope he'd picked out something special just for her? And, if that something was tied to a question, it might mean… Ventura stopped herself, not even daring to wish for it. She'd wanted Richard for so long, it seemed impossible to believe that he might want her too. In a lasting way. A way that meant forever. Ventura's lips quaked as she spoke.

"Should I open it?"

"I wish you would."

Ventura slipped off the silky red ribbon then unwrapped the pretty white package. She lifted the lid off the box, finding a cellophane-wrapped fortune cookie nestled inside.

"What's this?"

"Ventura Hart," he said, meeting her eyes, "from the moment I met you, I knew you were different. You made an impression on me the first night we met and then again on the Metro. The funny thing is, I bet you didn't believe me when I said I had this."

He pulled a small icon from his pocket and displayed it in his palm. It was a real four-leaf clover, wrapped securely in clear scotch tape.

"You weren't kidding?" she asked, delighted.

"I found this when I was eight years old. It was the year that Jenny was born. My parents were so happy then. Our whole world was golden. That was before my mom got sick, and Dad lost his way."

"I'm sorry," she said, her heart aching for him.

"But that's not why I'm telling you this. It's not to bring you down. It's to assure you that my hanging on to this meant I understood this sign was hopeful. I remember, Ventura, what a happy home life was like. I always wanted that for myself, and now…" He paused a beat. "I want it with you. We're right for each other, you and I. Two crazy, superstitious people who, on the outside, appear so levelheaded and together. But on the inside, we both want to believe in the same thing. That there's someone special out there for us, our missing other half."

She looked down at the fortune cookie, a lump welling in her throat. Richard nodded in encouragement and she ripped open the cellophane, popping the tiny crescent apart. Her fingers trembled as they held the fortune and she read it aloud. *"You are doomed to be happy in wedlock.* I can't believe that you found this," she said, meeting his eyes.

"I didn't," he replied with a soulful look. "I had it made."

"You what?" Tears streamed down her cheeks. "But why?"

"You had it with you that day on the train. The fortune was brittle. I could tell you'd had it for a while. Nobody carries something like that around unless it means something to them. Now, I know—to most folks—*doomed* might sound like a bad thing…" His eyes sparkled. "But something tells me you didn't take it that way."

"You really do know me," she said, her voice cracking.

"All I'm asking for is the chance to get to know you better—for many more years to come." He took a ring box from his pocket and pried it open. "I want to do this right, Ventura. For us to be a family."

Ventura stared down at the gorgeous solitaire glistening in the sunlight. "Richard, I can't believe that you'd—"

"Believe it. Please believe it…" He plucked the ring from its pillow and positioned it over her hand. "And then please say yes." He dove into her eyes and Ventura's heart melted. "You can work anywhere in the world you want," he said. "At the end of each day, just promise you'll come home to us."

She nodded, smiling through her tears, as he slid the ring on her finger. "I promise," she said in a shaky whisper.

Richard cradled her head in his hands, threading his fingers through her hair. His mouth met hers, and it was sheer heaven. Everything she'd longed for—his love, his sweetness and passion—came out in his kiss.

Something knocked loudly from down below. "Hey! Can we come up now?" It was Mary's voice, calling from the hull.

"Wow," Richard said with a laugh. "I'd nearly forgotten." He gave Ventura another peck on the lips and glanced at her ring finger. "You won't regret this," he said, heading for the cabin door.

To her amazement, Richard opened it, and Mary and Jason climbed up the ladder. Jason was carrying a big bag of Chinese food, as Ricky and Elisa followed.

"I knew it!" Ventura proclaimed with a happy laugh. "I knew I'd smelled pork lo mein!"

"Plus, extra fortune cookies," Mary said with grin.

Jason glanced at Ventura's finger, then gave Richard a way-to-go smile. Mary stepped onto the deck in high heels, carting champagne. "I'm so happy for you, Ventura. The paper will go on without you, but something tells me a family in Old Town can't."

Jason handed the bag of take-out to Richard, who held it toward the others. "Anybody hungry?"

"Yeah!" Ricky and Elisa cried.

As Ventura started to extract take-out cartons from the sack, the boat rocked.

"Here, let me help," Richard said, thrusting his hand in the bag.

"That's all right. I've got it."

"No, really!"

They both tugged at the bag, and it tore down the middle. Cartons sloshed sideways and spilled open, drenching both of their life vests. Ventura and Richard stared down at their soiled clothing and burst out laughing.

"*Doomed* may be right!" Richard said with a hoot.

Ventura hugged him tightly in spite of his messy apparel. "I love you so much."

He gazed down at her with adoring eyes. "I love you too."

The kids bounded toward them with giddy hoots and hollers, hugging them happily as well.

"What happened to Jason and Mary?" Ventura asked.

Richard motioned with his chin toward the bow of the ship, where Mary and Jason stood engaged in a rapturous kiss. "I guess they were inspired by the moment."

"Yes." Ventura studied Mary's four-inch heels, thinking she'd never learn how to dress for the outdoors.

Just then, a motor boat tore by, kicking up wake and sending their sailboat rocking.

"Whoa… Oh!" Mary cried, clinging on to Jason when her teetering heels began to slide.

"I've got ya," he said, holding her fast. But then his footing slipped as well. Ventura's eyes went wide as the couple swayed first to the left, then to the right. "Oooh! Whoa!" Then, *splash*! They flipped over the edge, resurfacing seconds later, bobbing about in their life vests. Mary sprayed Jason with water, laughing heartily. "You look terrible!"

He splashed her back. "Your mascara's running."

"Oh no!" She raised her hand to her face in horror, wiping black streaks from her cheeks.

"You know what?" Richard whispered to Ventura. "I'll bet he likes her better that way."

"How do you know?" she answered with a laugh.

He jostled her in his arms, the kids still clinging tightly. "That's when I fell for you."

"At the Tidal Basin?"

He nodded. "Both times."

She grinned shyly, finally admitting the truth. In some ways, Ventura felt like she'd been in love with this man forever. "I fell for you *way* before that."

He sexily cocked an eyebrow. "Really?"

"On that very first night."

His face warmed in a pleased expression. "I'm glad."

Ventura glanced at Mary and Jason, still frolicking in the water. "Should we help them back aboard?"

"In a minute," Richard said, giving her a kiss.

Little Elisa looked up. "Does *this* mean you're getting married?"

Ricky gazed up with a hopeful expression.

Ventura felt a smile tugging across her lips as she and Richard prepared to answer together. "*Yes!*" they shouted amid squeals and happy laughter.

"We love you, Ventura," Elisa said.

She looked down at the little girl and her brother, who also nodded.

"We really do," Richard told her. "All of us do."

Ventura held them tighter, fearing her heart might explode from the sheer joy of the moment. She was doomed to an eternity of happiness, and had been destined all along to become a part of this family. She absolutely, positively believed it. While she'd never precisely been lucky, her fortunes had begun to change the moment she'd met Richard. He'd brought luck and love and laughter into her life, and she planned to spend the rest of hers letting him and his wonderful kids know how much she adored them.

"Oh, Elisa, Ricky, Richard," she said with a sigh, "I love all of you back."

The End

A Note from the Author

Thanks for reading *My Lucky Groom*. I hope you enjoyed it. If you did, please help other people find this book.

1. This book is lendable, so loan it to a friend who you think might like it so that she (or he) can discover me, too.

2. Help other people find this book: write a review.

3. Sign up for my newsletter so that that you can learn about the next book as soon as it's available. Write to GinnyBairdRomance@gmail.com with "newsletter" in the subject heading.

4. Come like my Facebook page: http://www.facebook.com/GinnyBairdRomance.

5. Comment on my blog: The Story Behind the Story at http://www.goodreads.com.

6. Visit my website: http://www.ginnybairdromance.com for details on other books available at multiple outlets now.